The MANY DEATHS of GEORGE ROBERTSON

The MANY DEATHS
of
GEORGE ROBERTSON

✧

George Little

Goose Lane Editions

Published with the assistance of the Canada Council and the New Brunswick Department of Tourism, Recreation & Heritage, 1990.

Book design by Julie Scriver
Cover art: "Mahoney's Beach, Evening," two-plate etching and aquatint by Anna Syperek
Printed in Canada by Wilson Printing

Canadian Cataloguing in Publication Data

Little, George, 1937-
The many deaths of George Robertson

ISBN 0-86492-124-1
I. Title.
PS8573.I87M36 1990   C813'.54   C90-097570-9
Pr9199.3.L57M36 1990

Goose Lane Editions Ltd.
248 Brunswick Street
Fredericton, New Brunswick
Canada E3B 1G9

These stories are for Pearl
who is not in them except for the love

✧

CONTENTS

✧

FOREWORD

✧

It is rare that a man can write successfully from the point of view of a woman. George Little does it convincingly in several of the stories included in this new collection, and especially so in "Marooned," a sad and compelling story of a courageous woman gone mad after a disaster at sea.

But then, George Little is a surprising man. A teacher and essayist, he was for many years an active political colleague who, unknown to me—and to others, I suspect—was also busy writing the stories included in this remarkable book. In fact, in this first published collection of his stories, George Little demonstrates an unusual capacity to place himself in many of life's most interesting and demanding situations.

In "Circles," he movingly describes the changes in the nature of relationships which occur when a woman's feelings, about a man who is not her husband, shift from admiration and friendship to sexual attraction. In "The Blue Harris Tweed Coat," the still presence of a woman rendered unconscious by a stroke is the occasion for a son to recollect unsparingly on his life, his personality, and his love for his mother. Like so many of history's sons, he learned as a boy that the best way to blunt a mother's anger for wrongdoing is to be first in contriving a story in which he appears to blame himself. In "Broken Teeth and Frosty Leaves," Little persuasively recounts the thought and action of an adolescent girl—perhaps as only a sensitive man with two daughters could possibly do. Throughout these stories, George Little demonstrates a mind as diverse in its interests as it is empathetic to what was once conveniently called the human condition.

Most of Little's stories engage the reader because they are honest and vivid recollections of unique illustrations of life's common experiences. Others are dependent on the special perspective of an immigrant or an experienced traveller. Although his affection for humanity is evident, he is not a woolly-minded sentimentalist. In "Polling List," one of only two stories dealing with his political experience, he coolly observes, "Her voice had the fierce conviction and total clarity that only the really crazy can muster."

George Little has already demonstrated his commitment to others by his teaching and his political activism. He has, however, escaped the potential confines of both. With these stories he reveals a sensitivity to language and a breadth of vision unrestricted by either the confines of ideology or the pedantry of the classroom.

I hope that these stories are read by many, for they give pleasure to those who see in good fiction an engaging path to the truth.

Ed Broadbent

KITES and MUSHROOMS

✧

When Father came home from the war with a medal and a limp to add to the natural distinction of his gait, I copied the way he walked as I tried to model all the rest of my behaviour on his. The others, Kate, Anne, Laura and Billy, all much older than I, were out at work by then, and I was the one left at home to go with him on his walks. Even without the limp, he must have had a way of walking that was all his own—with a roll of the shoulders, and a twitch of the left foot which became almost a deformity in running. We all have it, we Duncans, and because of my special version of it, in later years my daughter Elspeth and her husband have taken to making fun of me when I run. They were amusing their daughter the other day when we were out flying a kite I had made her—impersonating me by bounding along in a strange lopsided way, leaning over to the left. She giggled when they zoomed down on her—and I must say I found it funny, too, though I'm sure they exaggerated. Even my Duncan run isn't all that grotesque.

Father used to take me for walks to watch the play on the village bowling green, and I learned to roll along with him as he limped up the hill from our house; that's why my walk is funnier than any of the others', I have always supposed. Even after the pain in his leg went away, it left a permanent stiffness; but it didn't keep him from bowling any more. I watched on my own from the edge of the green.

There was magic for me in those visits to the bowling—the bools, my father called it. The lawn was a beautiful green carpet, meticulously kept and zealously guarded by Tam Jardine, the green-keeper. No-one wearing hard, heeled shoes would have dared walk on it, for Tam had a sharp tongue given to withering scorn; all the bowlers wore soft leather shoes with flat soles—and he kept even the sloping, shallow banks like velvet. Between the banks and the green was a ditch filled with rounded white stones, where bowls not in play, their polished surfaces undamaged by the smooth pebbles, lay on their flat sides. The bowling club was quiet and private behind a high, close-knit hawthorn hedge; and its own noises were kept enclosed from the tennis club on one side and from the village cross-roads on the other. Past the church and the graveyard on the other side of the bottom hedge, in the distance across the Clyde valley the high Lanarkshire moors, warted with the black cancerous bings of abandoned coal mines, stretched away into rural Ayrshire. The sounds of the place were special—the soft wooden resonance of bowl on bowl, the even softer click of a bowl on the jack, the small white target ball; advice called from one end of a rink to another—"A wee bit tichter, Wullie—see if you can get roon that yin and we'll lie three"; sometimes cries of disgust for a bad shot— "Ye're awa' tae Kilcaigie wi' that yin—" implying that the bowl was way off course and seemed bound for a neighbouring village if the bank didn't stop it. Laughter, softened by the absorbing lawn, mingled with restrained cries of triumph. There was the soft padding of the supple bowling shoes down the green, as bowlers followed a shot down, often leaning over to encourage the biased bowl to take the desired path towards the jack. My father's limping steps had a rhythm peculiar to him, and his run was more lopsided than most, so that the skip of his cloth cap gradually worked its way round to end up ludicrously perched over his ear. Bending down and straightening up in the action of delivery must have been a real effort for him, but he seemed to manage it with enthusiasm, often stopping half-way down the rink to lean over, waving his arms in an almost mystic attempt to influence the curving course of the bowl. Between ends, or between games, he would sit with me on one of the wooden benches on the pink gravel path that enclosed the green, or on the sticky varnished seats in the musty-smelling club-house. Sometimes he would hold one of the bowls in his big dry hands, thoughtfully rubbing its sheen, cradling its weight as though already playing the next shot in his mind. I liked to trace on the ivory disk in the centre of the flat side of the bowls his carved initials, A.J.D., for Andrew James Duncan, his name and mine. When we sat outdoors, he would break off a hawthorn shoot from the hedge behind us and chew it in the corner of his mouth, and I would copy him, enjoying the sweet taste of the tender, pink tip. Much later I learned that he chewed the hawthorn shoots as a substitute for the cigarettes he would like to have smoked, but often could not afford to buy. He turned all the wages he earned as a hospital porter over to Mother's wise management, and settled for a small allowance of pocket money for himself.

It was on our walks to and from the bowling green that I unconsciously developed my own version of his sailor's roll and limp. Before the war he was called Farmer in the village, not because he ever worked on a farm for more than a few days at harvest time, but because he walked like a ploughman following a horse-drawn plough down a field. But after the war everyone called him Sailor, less in tribute to his war service than in half-jest about his exaggerated shipboard roll.

Those times are precious to me in memory because they mark the closest I ever came to knowing and loving him. I was only two when he went off to serve in the Navy, not, I am sure now, because the propaganda stirred up in him any strong sense of patriotism but rather because the war offered him steady employment and an opportunity to send home a regular pay to my mother. He had been a sailor in the First War too, and had learned skills in mine laying and mine sweeping; but between the wars he had long spells of unemployment after the district's coal mines closed down, and the family, before I came along, went through some hard times. Then with the war the skills they had taught him became valuable again. The authorities which had been quite willing to abandon him and his family to welfare lines and soup kitchens between the wars suddenly found that they could afford to pay him a living wage, and he could not afford to thumb his nose at them. So he volunteered, for he was too old to be conscripted, and I was left during the years of my earliest consciousness to the care of my mother and sisters and the strained tolerance of my brother. I was thoroughly spoilt. My mother especially made me the focus of her life, lavishing the affection on me that would, but for his absence in the cold, grey North Sea, have been shared with my father. At first when he came home, smelling of hospital disinfectant, antiseptic ointment, hair cream and full strength cigarettes, his fingers stained brown with nicotine, I resented him as a rival for her affection. The roughness of his sailor's flannel pants against the tenderness of my bare legs as I sat on his lap was a symbol for me of the threat he presented; his figure, bent over the heavy, thorn-wood walking-stick with its polished handle-knob, haunted my dreams and frightened me. I often woke up at night to his coughing—a throaty rasping that would pause in the dark only long enough for him to suck in the first drag on his cigarette, and then would burst out again worse than ever. It must have been then that my determination never to smoke was formed.

He would never have tried to buy my affection with chocolate and candies even if, in those days of rationing, he could have bought any; but by adopting me as his companion on his walks, he won me over without knowing it, and I grew desperate to impress him, to win his love. My boyhood skills, never as strong as brother Billy's, didn't seem to mean much to him; I wasn't much good at birdnesting or playing soccer—he would have called it fitba'—and even where I did excel, in all my school work, he heard my lessons without much enthusiasm and rarely praised my successes.

The walk I copied was the only part of him that stayed with me as I grew out of boyhood. My mother remained my favourite, and he still intimidated me, just a little. The only time in my adult life I can remember hugging him—I was returning from a two-year absence studying on a scholarship at the Sorbonne, a twenty-two-year-old who had learned something of the importance of physical contact—he was stiff and awkward and embarrassed, and I never tried again. I grew away from him, through education and travel, more than I did from any of the rest of the family. He alone of all of them showed no pride in my academic accomplishments, and no interest in my career as a writer in Canada. I sensed a deep resentment in him of the changes in my dress and speech and ideas. It was as though he felt I was becoming different from him out of spite, just to show him how inferior he was; our arguments about politics and religion became so bitter that we came to avoid the subjects altogether. He regarded my mid-Atlantic speech as showing off and my expensive clothes as needless waste. He would never accept the offers Susan and I made to pay his and Mum's fares to fly to Montreal to see us, and when we took trips home he was distant with all of us, even Elspeth, and could only with difficulty be persuaded to come with us on outings like picnics. Elspeth was troubled by him, not frightened as I had been, just a bit hurt that he didn't seem to like her very much. Until the day of the kite and the mush-rooms.

One day two years or so after Mum died, we were all together in Father's cramped living room. Our conversation seemed to swirl around him as he sat on his favourite armchair watching horse-racing on television, his stiff leg stretched awkwardly as always in front of him, a constant danger to anyone who wanted to squeeze past. My sisters and my wife Susan had cleared away the meal—that's how things were done in our house, always, and Susan accepted it, in spite of herself, with mild amusement. We men, Billy and I, and my youngest sister Laura's husband George, were talking about men's things—-the gardens, soccer—trying without much success to bring Father into the conversation from time to time with references to the horses. Only Laura and I had married; Kate and Anne seemed confirmed in their single existence, and Billy's ba-chelorhood was fixed in stone, a family joke. Laura and George had no children so Elspeth was the lone grand-child; she had many cousins on Susan's side of the family and, despite usually being the centre of attention when my family gathered, she often seemed lonely.

She was reading that day, in a corner by the piano, a colourful book about a Chinese family that her Aunt Kate had bought her; when she came to some pages with pic-tures of kites, she brought them in excitement to show us. There were brilliantly painted dragon kites and bird kites, flying against a deep blue sky.

"Look at these, Auntie Kate, aren't they pretty, aren't they?"

Kate showed the book to Father. "Remember the kites you used to make, Dad, for Anne and Laura and me, and we used to fly them down in Miller's field? Your Grandpa used to make kites that would fly higher than the birds,

Elspie—higher than these ones, I'll bet. You should ask him if he would make you one."

I nodded to Elspeth, in response to her questioning look, and she went over shyly to Father's chair. "Would you make me a kite, Grandpa, would you, like the ones in the book? I've never had a kite." He stirred uncomfortably in his chair.

"I wouldn't know how, anymore; it's been years since I made one." It came out more gruffly, through his breathy wheezing, than he intended, and he tried to soften the rejection. "How old would you have been then, Kate, eight or nine was it?"

"It was before Drew was born anyway, and Billy was just a baby, but I'm sure you haven't lost your touch. What was it you used to use—brown paper and a piece of split cane—surely we can find some of those in the back-room closet, and we can make some flour-and-water paste for glue if you don't have any of the white stuff. Come on, Elspeth, we'll go and look." She led my skipping daughter down the hallway to the bedroom.

"You don't have to bother, Dad, if you'd rather not," I said when they disappeared. "I'll buy her one tomorrow." He eased his stiff knee away from the front of his chair and pushed himself up, resting his weight on the padded arms. Even that small effort was enough to make him breathe very hard.

"Do you mean you've never made her one? It surely wouldn't be too much bother to make one better than these cheap things in the stores—they just tear in the lightest breeze. The lassie needs a good, strong home-made one she can paint herself." He was already limping his way through the squeaky kitchen door. "I've got some glue in here somewhere, no need for flour and water, just a mess. Some paints somewhere, too." Susan said quietly, "Let him do it, Drew. Elspeth would love him to make her something."

When the kite was finished—it was a simple design, with a spine and bowed head of split cane held together with string lashing and covered with brown wrapping paper shaped to fit and glued in place—Elspeth and her Aunt Kate drew fantastic swirls and circles on it and painted them purple and green and red with some poster paints Father found in a kitchen cupboard. And while they were doing this, Father carefully made the tail, a series of just the right number of paper bows tied on to a long piece of string that was essential for the kite's balance, and prepared the flying twine by winding it round and round the handle of a wooden spoon. Kate protested after it was all done that she was tired, and said, with a warning glance to me, that Elspeth and her Grandpa would have to go down the field themselves to fly it. Elspeth's disappointment at this was remarkably short-lived and she trotted off with Father, holding the kite while he carried the tail.

The two of them were gone for a good three hours, and I was just about to go to fetch them home for supper when the door opened and Elspeth bounded in holding the kite in one hand with its tail looped over the other arm. I don't think I ever saw her so excited.

"Mummy, Daddy, you should have been there; this is the best kite in the whole world. Grandpa showed me how to make it dance and it went up as high as it could go, right to the end of the twine; oh it was beautiful." Her face glowed and her eyes sparkled. She ran back to greet Father as he came through the doorway, breathing heavily, but with a spring to his limp I hadn't seen for years. His face had some of its sailor's flush, too, replacing the miner's grey that it had settled into in recent years.

"That was the best fun, wasn't it, Grandpa, making our kite dance? Let me take the mushrooms to Mummy." She

ran in this time holding her grandfather's big white handkerchief tied up at the corners into a bag. "See, Mummy,
Grandpa found mushrooms in the field and I found some
too, but he said they weren't good ones only the white
ones were good, see, they're in the hankie." Susan took
the handkerchief and undid the knots. The five mushrooms were beautiful, white plates, four inches across,
with subtle pink flesh on the underside; I remembered
Father bringing some home like this years before, and
knew he would cook them under the toasting grill, with
a big daub of butter in the centre of each one. No food
has ever tasted so delicious since.

As I tucked her into bed that night Elspeth was still
bubbling with her day. "Did Grandpa ever make you a
kite, Daddy, when you were little?" He hadn't, probably
because running after a kite in a rough pasture then would
have extended him more painfully than running after
bowls on a smooth green, even though the emphysema
hadn't started to limit his breathing.

"I don't think so, unless I was too young to remember.
We did pick mushrooms a couple of times though, and
brought them home in his hankie, just like today. Weren't
they the best mushrooms you've ever tasted?"

She turned over, sleep beginning to claim her. "Oh, yes,
they were just scrumshie. You can come and see Grandpa
make the kite dance tomorrow, Daddy." But it had rained
the next day, and the day after we had to drive to Pres-
twick for the flight back to Mirabel.

We didn't get back to Scotland for his funeral; ten years
passed before we could make the trip home and I went
to search for his gravestone in the cemetery behind the
church. We stayed with Kate in the old house, but I went
on my own to the graveyard—Susan, understanding, had
gone off with Elspeth to see her Aunt Laura. Although I
thought I would remember where the family plot was

from our visits after Mother's death, the outline of the cemetery had changed in the twelve or so years since I was last there, and I had to ask the gardener in charge to look up the family plot number for me. I passed several graves of people with familiar names from my past—Fred McRae the church organist, Johnny Smillie my Sunday School teacher, Old Mrs. Callan my parents' neighbour for thirty years, Tam Jardine the keeper of perfect lawns under unkempt sod—before I came to the simple grey headstone of polished granite at my father's and mother's grave. On the white facing-plate with their dates it said only in plain, black letters,

> IN LOVING MEMORY OF MARY ELIZA-
> BETH JOHNSTONE, BELOVED WIFE OF
> ANDREW JAMES DUNCAN; ALSO THE
> ABOVE ANDREW JAMES DUNCAN.

My father's name—and my name too. I shivered even in the warm sunshine, feeling cold, damp earth on my flesh, and mushrooms sprouting between my toes. The rows of graves stretched past the stone wall that used to separate them from Miller's field, and over the hazy valley beyond them I could see the distant moors; to my surprise, I noticed that all the dark tumours of bings had been cleared away by some massive environmental surgery. From the other side of a familiar hawthorn hedge where players prepared for a new game, I could hear the soft rumble and knock of bowls being swept together bumpily, end over end.

JACK PATRICK'S STORY

✧

The four of us—me, my brother Joe, the wife's brother Pete Ward and Frank Gill—used to go up country moose hunting every year to Pete's camp, in by Summerhill Lake. Pete's boss in the refinery sold him the lot cheap, and we all helped him put the camp on it. He's a big, clumsy guy, Pete, not much of a hand with a saw or a hammer, but Frank Gill's a carpenter by trade, works with a French outfit building houses on spec out by Westfield, and Joe's a good plumber, even though he is just a ticket agent with VIA. I did the wiring; even though the camp is away off the hydro line, it wouldn't have made any sense not to wire it, because, as I told Pete, you could always hook up your own generator, and anyway you never knew when they would open the lake up as a subdivision and bring the power in.

We could always count on one of us getting a Moose licence in the draw, and if we didn't, we always knew somebody who did that we could ask to come along with us. But this one year none of us got one and we were stuck for someone else to ask; it seemed that all the licenses went to Moncton that year. Then, nearly at the last minute I was talking to Bert Patterson in the Co-Op, and he happened to mention that he had got a licence, and didn't have anyone to go with. "I usually go up to Lil's Uncle Cecil's place, back of Sussex," he told me, in that funny high-pitched voice of his that some folk can't stand, "but the roof fell in last winter, and he never got round to fixing it. I was just going to drive up every day next week, but it's not so much fun on your own." I knew Bert, kind of, from playing hockey in the same league away back, and

I'd wired up a house for his old man a couple of summers before. I didn't know him well, you understand, though Sarah knew his wife Lil, and didn't think very much of her. But I phoned up the others to see if it was all right to ask Bert to come with us, and they said sure, if I thought he was O.K. And that was that, more or less. We just included him every year after that.

And it was fine, eh, at first. Plenty of room in Pete's cabin for the five of us—really we built it as a complete house, with a big front room looking onto the lake; Joe had even rigged up piped-in water from a spring up the hill, and put in a flush toilet when he was at it—Bert was real tickled with that, said it was better than Lil's Uncle Cecil's place, where you just had to go in the woods—and I rigged up a generator, one of these Japanese jobs, to give us power. Those first couple of years Bert fitted in fine, nothing crazy about him. Matter of fact, he was real good company. Played not a bad hand of poker. Kept us in stitches with funny stories about his wife Lil and her Holy Roller relatives. We'd often be sore laughing about the tricks her uncle Cecil would get up to, sneakin' out to the barn after the Wednesday night services in their kitchen for a couple of belts where her aunt couldn't see him. Seems once he got his quart bottle mixed up in the dark with a specimen he'd taken from his young gelding for the vet to examine, and swore off the drink for good. We used to laugh as much at Bert's funny voice, imitating Lil's relatives, as at what he was telling us. "It was a warning from the Lord, Bert, that's what it was; the Lord works in mysterious ways his wonders to perform, even with horse piss."

Bert said his wife's whole family practically worshipped the gelding after that; he said if the accident had happened a couple of years earlier it would still be a stallion.

The first year we noticed anything different—it would be the third or fourth, eh?—was after Lil caught the religion real bad herself. Led Bert a miserable life, and didn't even want him to come with us that year at all. She did warn him off the drink though, said she wouldn't have him in the house with the devil's breath on him, and I guess when he was home he did what she said. He looked real down the couple of times I saw him at the Co-Op that summer, but none of us had any idea it would take him that bad—I suppose you never know.

I never saw such a change in a man, that hunting season. We were up there for a week, and he never drew a sober breath from one Friday to the next. He'd brought about five forty-ouncers of Captain Morgan with him in a green sports bag, and he drank more than half of one every night, when we were through for the day. Mostly, see, we stuck to beer, or the odd rye, but we'd never seen his like for drinking. He wouldn't play cards; after the first couple of nights he was in no fit state to play anything, anyway; and when he near blew a hole in the gate of the half-ton—that would be the Wednesday—we took his gun away from him. From then on all's he did was lie on his bunk, just a pitiful sight altogether. He was bitchy at first, then moody, then he just lay there moaning one minute and laughing the next, then crying and promising Lil he'd never do it again. It made us grouchy too, the rest of us, with him and with each other; especially me, since I kind of felt responsible for him; especially Frank, too—it was his father's half-ton.

His rum was all gone by the Friday, and he slept from about breakfast time right through to Saturday noon. You should have heard him when he woke up, swore he didn't remember a thing about the whole week, thought he had been sick all the time; well, what could we do, we just had to go along with him. He said he felt fine now—you'd have thought he would have had the worst hangover, but he didn't have as much as a sore head. In fact, he was all for staying another day to make up for lost time, but we talked him out of that pretty quick.

He was on the wagon all the next year, or so everybody said, and when it came to Moose time again, we thought he would be all right, eh? Such a decent big fella, he was, when he was sober, we all liked him; to tell the truth we were sorry for him, seeing the dog's life that Lil led him. About the only pleasure she left him with was the hunting, and she wasn't too keen on that. She told the wife that she only let him go with us because she knew we were decent, and not up to any foolishness. And you know, it was the same as the year before—worse, if anything, because he brought more rum this time, and drank it faster. It was the remorse that was the worst, after the rum was finished, lying in his bunk sobbing and moaning like Jimmy whatsisname on the T.V. after they caught him with that woman. "Oh, I've sinned, I've sinned," and "I'm not good enough for you, Lil," he was just whining, over and over again. It was enough to make you sick, it really was, and it made us determined to have no more to do with him.

The following year the four of us made up our minds to leave him out—I got a licence myself that year in the draw. They left it to me to tell him, but I kept putting it off, hoping maybe he wouldn't want to come anyway; but wouldn't you know—the day we were in the Co-Op stocking up for the camp, didn't he come right up and put down his usual share of the groceries money. I mean, what could I do—I couldn't just tell Bert we'd had enough of him, you just can't, eh, not on a stone-cold sober Thursday afternoon. As I say, he's not the kind of fella you want to be mean to, and there was that trouble with his wife and her religion. Anyway, the end of it was that he came along with us that year too. I think if Frank Gill had had his rifle with him that day I'd be speaking with a kind of high-pitched voice myself now, if you know what I mean.

It started raining just as we arrived at the camp, and it never let up all week. There were high winds, too; cold and miserable it was, more like early December than September; one day we even had sleet. We never got out of the cabin, hardly, just played cards, drank a lot of beer—Joe said it was the only Moose we were going to see that year. Well, you may as well laugh, eh? At first Bert was fine, too, didn't drink at all, and was back to tellin' funny stories about Lil's relatives. He gave us quite a demonstration of their services—a lot of shouting and eye-rolling and falling about on the floor. I remember even Pete saying it was just like the old days.

Then about Wednesday he started into the rum—I don't know how many he had with him, but his bag looked awful heavy when he brought it out. More than enough, anyway. By the time we turned in that night, he was pretty near miraculous—he had quite a time getting into bed, but he fell asleep right away. We thought that was a good sign. The next day it was the same—never quit drinking all day, just kept tossing it back, one glass of neat rum after the other. He wouldn't listen at all when we tried to warn him he'd had enough; him such a skinny big rake you wouldn't have thought he could take what he did without falling over, but by night time he was still knocking it back when all the rest of us went to bed.

The middle of the night, I woke up to this god-awful thumping and crashing. In the light from the fire embers I could just make out Bert tramping around the floor with these great big clogs on his feet; he was muttering something about having to go, and not knowing where the bloody place was. When I dragged myself out of bed and over to him, I could make out what his trouble was; he had stepped into two empty twelve-pack boxes in the dark, and was dancing around with one on each foot, without the sense to kick them off. Aside from the boxes he didn't have a stitch of clothes on.

I helped him out of them, and steered him to the toilet, in by the kitchen—like I say, it's a real posh place, Pete's camp. As I was getting him back to his bunk, the other three were sounding real owly about the row, so I told them to shut up and go back to sleep, and went back to bed myself.

It didn't take me long to doze over, but I must have had one ear kind of half-open, because a while later—it must have been an hour or so, I suppose—I woke up again. I could hear the rain just pelting down on the roof and against the windows, and at first I thought that was what had wakened me; then I heard this weird slapping and a muffly kind of moan—it was a bit scary in the dark. Joe must have heard something too, because I heard him stirring around for his flashlight, a big square one he got through his work with the railroad. As I sat up, he flicked it on and did a sweep round the room. I whispered "What is it, Joe?"

"I dunno." The beam swivelled past Bert's bunk, then quickly back. It was empty. "Where the hell—he's not there." Joe sounded some disgusted. "What in hell's he up to now? Get up and see if he's in the john, will you?"

My feet were half off the bunk when I caught sight of this shadow against the big window. I drew my legs up again, and whispered, "Joe, what's that—over by the window. Shine the light—no, the picture window. For the sake of—"

In the beam, and through the reflection, there was a sight I'll never forget. Stretched out against the window was this bedraggled-looking thing, shivering, naked, arms and legs pressed against the glass—all the rest of him against it too, as near as he could manage. He was like some kind of a crucifix in a display case. Most of him was shrivelled up, you know, from the cold, for the rain was beating down harder than ever, and he must have been frozen, his hair plastered down to his skin like that. We could see his lips moving, but could hardly hear him pleading to be let in.

"Leave the stupid son of a bitch out there all night," Pete said from his bunk, "it'll serve him right." He never did like being disturbed in his sleep, and this was the second time in the one night. "He must have got lost looking for the john again," I said, "and locked himself out. What a state he's in." Joe saw the funny side of it. "God, if anyone ran into him, wandering around like that out there, they'd think he was some kind of monster, the old man of the woods or something." Frank Gill mumbled something, then laughed out loud. "The Summerhill Sasquatch, more like." Joe was tickled with that, and he was still laughing all the time we were towelling Bert down—we couldn't really leave him out all night like that. Until we got him stuffed into his sleeping bag he kept muttering about going in the trees, and not telling Lil. Then he gave a crazy laugh, and gradually his teeth stopped chattering; there was one big shiver, and we heard no more from him all night. The rest of us settled back to sleep, but I heard Joe laughing quietly to himself. "Summerhill Sasquatch, that's rich."

We had some laugh about it on the Friday with Bert taking some rough razzing. Joe had no mercy on him at all, giving him a real hard time about the twelve-pack clogs, and how puny certain parts of him had looked against the glass. Said he had never known before the rain could shrink them like that. Bert, though—he didn't remember a thing about it, and said we were just making it up—didn't take kindly to us calling him Sasquatch at all, and just got drunker than ever that night. As a matter of fact, we were all so fed up with the weather that we all had a bit too much, otherwise we would never have gone along with this crazy scheme of Frank Gill's.

He got a piece of leader—off a fishing line on an old rod that Pete kept in the camp—and tied it round Bert's big toe, once he was sound asleep; real funny-shaped big toes he had, kind of like claws, splayed out and crooked. As he was tying it, Frank was laughing, and saying that if Bert had left any footprints out in the mud, it would look right enough as if a monster had been on the prowl round the camp. Anyway it made it easy for Frank to get a good grip with a loop of line—and he was none too gentle with it either. Then he slipped the reel back on the rod, and stood it up by his own bed. Now Bert was out cold, so he didn't move much, just snored like a pig lying on his back. But every time he stirred the ratchet on the reel would click out a few notches; the rest of us just doubled over at that. Every click would send us into fits— you know how it is when you're hysterical drunk—and trying to keep quiet only made it worse. "Just let the dumb bastard try to go on the tear tonight," Frank wheezed out between spasms, "I'll reel him in like a trout. I've never yet let one away that big." Pete was in pain. "When's the Sass, the Sass, the Sasquatch season?" By the time he got this sneezed out he was on his knees, holding his ribs, with the tears rolling down his cheeks. "He'd look good stuffed," and he was gasping for air at this, "over the bar in the rec room." And that set us all off again.

Even when we crawled into our bunks, just bushed, we nearly wet ourselves every time Bert moved and the reel gave a rickety click; but pretty soon we were all sound asleep. He likely wouldn't have wakened us if he had set the camp on fire. As it happened, he didn't move till morning—not that we knew of anyway. But you should have seen him hopping around the floor with his pants down round his ankles trying to get the line off his toe. Even hung over, we got a big charge out of that—funny enough he had a wicked hangover too. His language must have scared away all the moose clear into Albert County, for we never saw a trace of one, even though it cleared up enough for us to be out after them all day.

That was Bert's last year of hunting with us, the poor devil. Got born again at a tent meeting up in Maugerville the next summer, and swore off the drink and card-playing for good. Then they moved away, Lil and him, to Oakville, that was a couple of years back, when there was a slack time and the mill was laying off. Never heard from them since. I see her Uncle Cecil every once in a while in the Co-Op, but he says he never hears much from them either. Cecil's back on the bottle again, I hear, but he tells me they say Bert still won't touch a drop. I wonder what the hunting's like, though, in that part of Ontario.

SOPHIE'S SONG

✧

The Friday four days from the end of the campaign in the very Conservative riding of York-Queens had been long and hot. Ben Killeen, the NDP candidate, had shaken countless hands and nodded to a hundred confidences. Although he was uncertain what effect such canvassing had on the way people voted, it was the part of politics he liked best; even so it was tiring, day after day. Easing himself between the sheets in the airless attic room, he let the day's encounters swirl around him; voices and faces blurred, came in waves, receded; scenes repeated themselves in clear detail, but in jumbled order. He punched the pillow, turned over on his back, kicked off the sheets, tried to shake the cramp from his feet and calves.

From downstairs he could hear Alan Gray, his campaign manager, and his wife, Tina, putting the house to bed; the clicks and squeaks of doors and windows closing punctuated the low rumble of their talk. He imagined they would be discussing their little girl Sophie's tantrum.

"I don't want you in here, Daddy. Leave me alone, leave me alone." Her four-year-old voice, forced out between sobs, had seemed much older. She had committed some rather serious crime much earlier in the day—long enough before bedtime at any rate for her to have forgotten the consequent penalty of no story. Alan had tried to explain the family judicial system. "Remember, Sophie, Mummy said no story tonight."

Because Tina was out with a client discussing a compensation case, there could be no appeal to her for clemency and the sentence had to stand. They had all three been to the doctor for needles that morning in preparation for a fall trip abroad, and Sophie was beginning to feel the effects; the discomfort in her arm, added to the obvious injustice of no story, outraged her; and she railed at her father. "Get out of my room! Get out of my room! I hate you Daddy, get out, get out!" And Alan, exhausted by the struggle even more than she was, had come downstairs leaving her crying bitterly. After fifteen horrid minutes when she showed no signs of easing her wails, Alan put down his book. "Ben, do you think you could do anything with her? I'm beat." He sounded it, too. "Sure," Ben had said, "I'll try. I may be a bit out of practice, but I've had to do a bit of work in my day on broken hearts at bedtime. Maybe I can settle her down." As he climbed the lovely dark oak staircase though, he had thought that his own two girls, now long grown up, had never had fits of temper quite like the sobbing Sophie's.

"Can I come in, Sophie? It's Ben." Through her sobs, she said something that wasn't no. "Do you want me to sit on your bed for a while?" Again the answer, though indistinct, was not a rejection. He sat on the quilted cover and stroked her dark head; the little brow was hot and flushed; and she trembled from the exertion of her sobbing—the kind of gigantic bodyquakes that only children seem capable of producing. Softly, fitting the tune to the rhythm of his stroking, he started to sing a Scottish lullaby, one he hadn't sung for twenty years:

> *Ho Ro, my nut-brown maiden,*
> *Hee ree my nut-brown maiden.*

Gradually the heaving shoulders calmed and quietened, and the sobbing gave way to more regular breathing and eventually to the deeper rhythm of sleep, broken ever more intermittently by shuddering sighs. Sure at last she was sound asleep, Ben arranged the sheet over her and went back downstairs, humming over the last line of the song—

For she's the lass for me.

"I think she'll be all right now, for the night. That needle really took it out of her," Alan had said gratefully. "You haven't lost your touch, eh? The old honey tones."

"Yeah," he said, "I'm glad they finally did some good today."

They had sat, sipping Irish Cream from tiny pewter goblets, enjoying the silence, or talking now and then about the campaign, how there was always something inexorable about these last few days, for people's minds were made up now, even if they hadn't been before. The party had never elected a New Brunswick M.P.; in fact, it was only recently that it had come to be regarded as any choice at all. Neither Ben nor Alan really expected to win this time either, though they both hoped to increase their vote considerably. The party was content with mainly moral victories in this province where people were fixed in their politics, by and large, as they were in religion, and getting them to change their vote was about as hard as getting them to change their seat in church.

Between mellow sips, Ben had tried to turn the conversation to some of the day's events. "That nursing home, the Manor, that's quite a place, isn't it? There's an old supporter over there, Peter Foster, did you ever meet him, Alan? He's been with the party, and the CCF before it, since the very beginning."

"I must get over to see him some day—he probably knows my Dad," Alan had said. "How would you like to spend your old age in a place like that?"

"Oh, as long as you had your faculties intact, it would be all right, I suppose, if you had to be in a home. But just imagine being stuck in a wheelchair, maybe after a stroke, or just senile, depending on some nurse for—well for everything, really. You should see some of these people, Alan."

Just then Alan had got up to listen at the foot of the stairs for Sophie, thinking he had heard her cry, and when he returned the subject of their talk had changed. Shortly after, Ben had come up to bed.

Now, as he listened to the comforting sounds of the old house shaking itself down for sleep, and tried to fit his own bones to the unaccustomed lumps of the guest bed, he thought of Sophie and her sobs and the song, and thought too of the only other time that day he had really felt useful.

Golden Years Manor, a low, modern nursing home, although on the other side of the river, was a part of the riding, and Alan had arranged for him to visit with the old people—*senior citizens* was their official category in the polling charts—who lived there. They were voters, after all, and they would appreciate meeting the candidate, even if they had always voted for one of the other two parties all their lives. One of the nurses, Ellen she was called, had been delegated to show him round, a briskly plump, cheerful woman in her mid-forties, efficient looking in her starched coat and cap. As they went, she explained the lay-out of the home. "We have two hundred in the Manor," she told him, "about half of them in one-room apartments; the other half need some kind of nursing care." Ellen seemed to know by name all of the people (what should he call them—guests? inhabitants? patients? inmates?), and could give him some brief biographical details as he went from room to room. "Hello, Bill," he would say, "good to see you today. Ellen here tells me you were out visiting your grand-daughter yesterday. How are things in Stanley?" And he shook dry old hands, repeating a few phrases sometimes for the hard of hearing. "I'm Ben Killeen, for the election you know? The election, on Monday?" and passed on to the next voter. Most were pleased to see him, and would have liked him to stay longer, though there were a few, Joe Harrison he remembered especially, who wanted nothing to do with him or the election or politics in general. "All the same, you blokes," Joe, a scrappy fox terrier of a man, had said, turning back to Bob Barker on television, "Just out for what you can get." Now and again he was gratified to come across a faithful supporter. "Been voting for you fellas since 1935—it's about time you stopped losin' my vote for me."

In one room a tall upright man in a green jacket patched with suede at the elbows and neat grey slacks was watering some plants on a sunny window ledge. There was something about him, even before he turned, something about the angle of his craggy head, that Ben found impressive.

"Here's somebody you'll be glad to see, Peter. He's a real expert on politics, aren't you Peter?" The gaunt frame swung around, and Ben was surprised to be recognized. "Well, come in Mr. Killeen, come in. Have a seat." His voice was clear and resonant, his grip firm. Ben sat on a straight, wooden chair, noting on the desk beside it a small typewriter bordered by neatly arranged sheets of paper and some pencils. On shelves above it were rows of books on political topics and Ben recognized some classics of the left from his own library.

"Doing some writing, are you, Peter?" he asked, nodding at the typewriter.

"Oh, I just peck away now and again at some memoirs, of the old days, you know. Nothing for showing anybody yet." The blue eyes twinkled behind half-glasses, and as they talked, Ben discovered that Peter Foster, who looked about seventy, was in fact nearly ninety.

"You'd better watch your reputation, all the same, Mr. Killeen, as a respectable candidate," Peter told him, with a wink to Ellen. Joining in his game, she teased him. "Been down visiting Alice MacDonald again, after curfew, have you?"

"No, no, talking with a jailbird, I mean. I went to jail in Winnipeg in 1919, with Woodsworth and those guys— said I struck a policeman. I told the judge I couldn't do that nightstick much harm with my head, but he gave me thirty days, anyway," and he laughed a warm, round laugh. Ben felt affection and admiration for this man, tinged with a kind of envy for the struggles he had been part of, the times he had lived through. It must have been easier somehow, he felt, when issues were clearer, when it was easier to tell "them" from "us."

He promised as they were leaving, Ellen having reminded him that they had better move on, to come back for a longer visit after the election was out of the way. "That won't be so easy though, with you in Ottawa." Peter's laugh this time was the kind one conspirator gives to another, as though he and Ben shared some secret hidden from Ellen. It made Ben feel oddly uncomfortable. "Good luck to you, anyway, Mr. Killeen. I'll send you a copy of my memoirs, care of the House of Commons. It'll save on the price of the stamps."

"Yeah, you do that, Peter. Take care of yourself—I'll see you again." As they left, Ellen smiled. "Growing old wouldn't be so bad if you could be sure of turning out like that, eh? Does your heart good, Peter does, just to talk to him." Part of Ben agreed.

At a turning in the corridor a tiny white-haired woman shuffled up to them. Clutching a worn, hand-knitted cardigan to her throat with blue-veined hands she peered directly into his face. "Do you know Percy Brown? He's my son, you know. I've been trying to phone him but—" she paused to recollect some strange puzzle. Even worried as it was, her voice had a soft, musical cadence. "I have to warn him not to come today. Did you hear about the bears? Maybe you could tell him for me—I heard it on the radio." She reached out to grasp his sleeve. "I've been trying to phone. There's these bears out there." Ellen gently broke her grip and took her by the elbow. "Come on Annie, let's get you back to your room. Mr. Killeen will see about the bears, won't you Mr. Killeen."

When she returned she told Ben that Annie Brown had not had one visit from her only son in four years. "She can't phone anymore, the new touch-tones, they puzzle her. Maybe just as well. Some families, eh?"

They had gone through the home—not such a bad place, Ben thought, certainly better than some others he had visited—until only one small wing remained. "There's not much point wasting your time down there," Ellen explained. "They're so far gone they wouldn't know you from the Prime Minister; they won't be voting, anyways." But Ben had asked to be taken through, and it was in the corridor he had met Mrs. Légère in her wheelchair. Her hair was a mere wisp of white, barely covering her skull, but her eyes were clear, and she was spry-looking in a blue dress—there were some strange, whirling, flame patterns of orange in the print. At her neck a silver crucifix glinted in the overhead lights. When Ben stopped to speak to her, ignoring a signal from Ellen which he did not quite understand, she answered him rapidly in French, and though Ben had spent some time as a teacher in an Acadian fishing village—his fluent bilingualism was one of the reasons the party had nominated him—he could make no sense of what she said. He drew up a stool to sit beside her, and held her hand in both of his, and slowly her babbling ceased. When he spoke to her gently in what had once been her own language she looked at him in surprise, tried a few phrases of nonsense in response, and then wept soundlessly. The tears coursed down her wrinkled face on to the blue of her dress, staining it, and when she lifted his hands to kiss them, the salt seemed to sear his skin. They sat there in silence until another nurse, taller and more angular than Ellen, arrived to wheel Mrs. Légère away for medication.

"There's some sad cases in here, too, that's for sure, Mr. Killeen," Ellen had said, as she walked him to the door. "But we do our best."

As she faded down the polished corridor, Ben's legs suddenly felt weak, and he slumped into a wheelchair by the door. It was an electric one, operated by a single control in the arm. Ben tried to stretch his fingers to the joy-stick, like one of those computer games, but he could not, and the effort exhausted him. He cried out for help, but only a stream of nonsense in a strange dialect, half-Scots, half-French, came out, echoing down the hall. A tall nurse bent down, laughing in his face, but he could make no sense of what she was saying. From behind him he could hear Ellen's voice. "A sad case, with the election on Monday, too." But he could not turn his body, or even his head, to see her. He reached desperately again for the control, but his stiff fingers slipped from it. Viciously taking his hand, the tall nurse jammed it on to the shiny knob so hard that the chair swivelled madly around and dashed wildly down the corridor. He heard Ellen's voice, still behind him, calling out "Couldn't tell you from the Prime Minister," and the other nurse's raucous laugh. All the way down the hall scaly claws were stuck out of the doors, and he tried desperately to shake every one as he rushed past, faster and faster. A melodious voice called gaily,

"Watch out for the bears." The chair swayed madly round a corner, and he was flying from it, two wet, wrinkled hands trying frantically to clutch him, a shining silver cross consumed in orange flames dazzling his eyes.

"Are you all right, Ben?" It was much like Peter Foster's voice, but it sounded so young. "Are you crying?"

He could only dimly make out the small outline against the doorway, backlit by filtered light from the street. "No, Sophie, I'm all right."

"Do you want me to sing you a song, Ben?" She padded over to the bed and put her hand into his. "No, thanks, Sophie," he whispered. "You'd better go back to bed. I had a nasty dream, that's all. Good night, now."

"Daddy says I have nasty dreams because I think too much. Do you think too much, Ben?" She was whispering too.

"I suppose so. Now go back to bed before you wake Mummy and Daddy up."

She tugged on his hand. "Will you take me back to bed, Ben, and sing me the nut brown song?"

When Sophie was asleep again, Ben made his way back to the guest room and into bed. After a few settling turns, he slept dreamlessly until morning.

The MANY DEATHS of GEORGE ROBERTSON

✧

When George Robertson died in Halifax, Nova Scotia, one day, nobody noticed. That's not so surprising as nobody had noticed all the other times either. For George, you should understand, had been dying or disappearing for years. It wasn't a gradual process; he didn't disappear, Cheshire-cat-like, bodily part by bodily part, until only a smile remained—it was more of a complete off and on process. From time to time he would notice that, physically, he just wasn't there anymore. The first few times he found it, as you might expect, a disturbing, not to say alarming, experience. He would be sitting somewhere, and suddenly he would just know that the seat he had been in, or the spot he had been standing on, was empty.

He remembered the very first time it happened, some months before they emigrated to Canada. It was in a bus one November evening, about half past five, going home from a late play practice, and a furtive meeting with Kirsty MacCallum, in the school in Oban—these were days in Scotland when teachers didn't own cars, as a general rule. He was sitting a few rows back on the driver's side facing the blinded window which separated the driving compartment from the rest of the bus, looking for his face which should have been reflected among the faces of the other passengers in the darkened glass. With something approaching panic, he realized that he could not see his own features; as he searched desperately through the heads in front of him, or in front of where he knew he had been, he could see everyone else's face but his own. Bill Brooks, the policeman in the village, head and shoulders above his pretty, pregnant wife—they were there, coming back from an afternoon's shopping in town. Drunkenly slouched against the side of the coach he could see was old Angus MacIvor, who always went in to collect his pension cheque the fourth Tuesday of the month, and always spent half of it in *The Hielan' Coo* before he got home. Even the conductress, Annie something or other (he remembered, as she stooped over his seat to collect the fares, smelling the vinegar from the fish and chips she had obviously just eaten before the bus left the depot), she was there, clearly reflected in the glass, her blue peaked cap held at its usual gravity-defying angle by an armory of hair-pins. But his own face was nowhere to be seen. There was the briefest moment when he was outside the bus, looking through the window, clawing desperately to get in to join all these people he so clearly recognized. He thought crazily that he must have missed the bus and that Alice would be worrying when he didn't get off at the top of their road with the other passengers from the village. Quickly he dismissed the silly notion, for he was, after all, on the bus; he could see everyone else even if he couldn't see himself; and when he looked in the glass again there he was right enough; there was no mistaking the bushy moustache underlining his bulbous nose, nor the green tweed deer-stalker hat, a minor affectation that Alice always teased him about.

It wasn't until the fourth or fifth of these disappearances that George started to make any systematic record of the phenomenon. He began to note down the occasions in a tiny spiral-bound notebook carried, with a thin red pencil stuck down the spine, in his inside jacket pocket. He even tried timing them, but he found that was impossible; the second hand on his watch, or the big sweep hand on the classroom clock, refused to register any passage of time during his absences. They often happened in school, in class; when his students were working on some writing exercise, or reading *Kidnapped* or *Quentin Durward*, the sensation of physical disappearance would come over him. It wasn't that he had any sense of having been transported to some other existence, he just wasn't anywhere as a physical being, as though he had been atomized where he sat. The fact that nobody else noticed ceased to puzzle him as soon as he realized that he was gone for only a fragment of a second; for the class it would be as though he had cut a single frame from a film and then spliced it together again, so that when he ran the film, *Great Expectations*, perhaps, or *Julius Caesar*, borrowed from the County Education Department in Dunoon, no-one could tell there was a frame missing. For any watching eyes his absences were as unnoticeable as the hundredth part of a blink.

And after the early shock, George grew to enjoy them. Although he could not make them happen at will, and was unable to forecast them, he began to look forward to them, to think of them as tiny holidays, a gift or visitation like the second sight of his seer-ancestors. He was tempted to tell Kirsty MacCallum, the girls' gym teacher, about the experiences, but he could not bring himself to. In the end, he told no-one about them, not even Alice, and only partly because he would have felt ridiculous trying to explain them. When they moved to Canada with their two daughters, Jennifer and Patricia, the absences continued for a couple of years. And then the big one took place, the one, George thought afterwards, that blunted his gift irreparably.

George Cormier, one of his colleagues on the staff of the fine new high school on the outskirts of Halifax where he had come to teach English, had been killed one morning in a dreadful road accident. When George arrived in school, a bit late and knowing nothing about it, the rest of the teachers were gathered in the staff room discussing the terrible details. Standing on the fringe of the group hearing them talk about their dead colleague in the hushed tones people use on such occasions, George suddenly disappeared again; only this time, just before he went, he was aware of something new and disturbing. The George they were talking about was himself. He was the one whose car had been mangled by a loaded oil-tanker on the off-ramp to the Mackay bridge. He wanted to cry out to them that he was there, but there was a barrier between them like a two-way mirror that he could not penetrate. At first he was angry at himself for having been so careless; he just couldn't have been paying attention to the road. Then he was overcome by fury at the injustice— why him, of all people; and finally, in the fraction of an instant before recall, he was consumed by sadness for his own loss, for the loss of Alice and Jennifer and Patricia, a grief he felt so intensely that, when he found himself back again, there were tears in his eyes, and he was sobbing. He seemed to have been gone for longer than usual, maybe for one-and-a-half frames this time. As they filed out of the room—school was cancelled for the day—he heard Mrs. Clark, the head of the Social Sciences department, whispering to the Physics teacher John Franklin; she had never known, she said, that the two Georges were so close.

Then the disappearances stopped, some block seeming to prevent them. George wondered anew what had caused them, what they had really been. Maybe, he thought, they were tiny images of death, and the shock of his colleague's violent end had somehow anaesthetized the faculty that governed them, the enormity of the real horror blotting out the imagined glimpses. His life was somehow duller without them, and he missed them, as though something had taken away, without warning or explanation, some privilege he had been enjoying. Since it had been a privilege he could not really complain—and who would he have complained to, anyway? But he felt its loss keenly nevertheless.

✧

"That's much better this week, Mr. Walker, much clearer. There are signs of progress there." Dr. Gagnon's gentle voice always seemed to me strangely incongruous for someone so obviously in control of her life. Her mannish haircut and square-cut tweed suit had intimidated me the first time I entered her office six weeks before, and still did, until she spoke; then her soft, melodic French accent charmed me and I lost my fear. But not enough to be able to shake off the black mood which had seized my life, not enough to reach through the death of the spirit that froze my tongue.

"Do you think this helps you, to write about yourself as though you were someone else?" she asked.

I reached over and tapped the ash off my cigarette, noticing that the quivering had nearly stopped today so that only a few pieces of ash missed the large glass ashtray. I desperately wanted to say "Yes, I used to do it all the time as a kid, fantasizing, you know? In my head I would hear the radio commentator's voice talking about me. It would be Gordon Walker, the first Scottish holder of the world mile record, or Gordon Walker, scoring the winning goal at Hampden against England before a hundred and twenty thousand roaring fans. I would rather have done that than anything." Instead I mumbled, "Don't know. Probably not."

She made a notation on the notebook before her, the busy scribble of her felt-tip pen making an irritating fingernail-scratching on the paper as it circled something she thought was important. "And how about death? You said that maybe these absences were somehow connected with death—was that ever a part of your fantasies?"

I sat back from the desk, and gazed at a flickering on the carpet. Shadows of the bare, clawing branches on the trees lining the hospital driveway outside did a macabre dance on the flame-red patterns. Flickerings inside my head copied the light and shade, the painfully bright colours and the moving, pleading fingers of the mocking boughs. Tom Sawyer coming back from the dead to be at his own funeral, hearing how good he had been—to come back when your death was still fresh in people's minds, when the awfulness of it still prevented them from dealing with the real you, and made them dwell instead on the ideal, half-remembered, half-created you; would that be out of fear of offending your still-hovering spirit, or in propitiation of an angry providence, quite likely to snatch them next. Or Frost's poem about swinging birches—to be away from life just long enough to see what death was like, and love life the more for it—that was always something I could relate to clearly, before my own shadows closed around me. But I had never been able to feel that my tiny disappearances were like that; for one thing they seemed to be totally involuntary, came to me unasked and left the same way. I reached again for the words to explain. "They're not the same." She smiled in a way that in anyone else would have seemed condescending. "For next week, tell me how."

✧

In the weeks that it took George to realize that his little holidays had stopped, he became harder and harder to live with. Alice had always complained that he never had enough to say to her, that he seemed to use up all his ideas on the people in school, as though she hadn't the intelligence to converse about anything important. He had never taken her half-joking complaints too seriously, and at other times she seemed quite pleased that they found no need for the empty talk with which some of their friends filled up their living together. But when the loss of his momentary escapes became an unbearable ache in him, he found it difficult to give more than grunted responses to Alice's questions, and he was less and less able to initiate any kind of conversation with her. At work he was able to play the role of teacher almost as before, especially in class before his students. But his colleagues must have noticed his long silences in the staffroom; most of them (if they bothered remarking about his silences at all) probably joked behind his back about male menopause.

It was Alice, though, who suffered most from his depression, and when she tried to talk him out of it, or to persuade him to seek help, it only became worse. "What have you got to feel down about?" she would ask, gently at first, but with increasing impatience. "Everybody loves you, you've got a job you like, we're very comfortable— oh, for God's sake, just give yourself a shake." As though he didn't know all this already, as though that guilt was not half the weight that pushed him down. Often at night she would snuggle up to him in bed, when he was pretending to be asleep, and he could feel her sobs through his back. They had always enjoyed sex together; especially after he had had one of his absences, George would be strong and tender in his love making, and Alice sometimes wildly responsive. Now he didn't have the interest; it was worse somehow, that he was not physically impotent, for erotic scenes in films or passages in books could still temporarily arouse him. But no matter what Alice did to stimulate him, their feeble attempts now ended in frustration and tears, until they gave up trying. The silence between them grew.

✧

"I don't know that you have answered my question, this week, Mr. Walker. There is, you know, a quite common idea that the sexual act, especially in its climax, is a kind of dying—*un petit mort*, we say in French. Would George have been aware of that, do you think? Could that have explained his, his failures with his wife?" She said "failures" apologetically, as though she would have liked to use a more precise word, but couldn't find one.

I had expected that our talks would get around to this sooner. Before my admission to hospital, I had had no previous experience with psychiatrists, but from my reading I thought they would eventually trace everything back to sex. Now I found it embarrassing, and looked away from her steady gaze before answering. "Yes, I suppose I—he—had heard the phrase. Isn't there an Edith Piaf song? But how would that—I mean—Ann—Alice—wasn't connected with the absences before; would she be, now?" I caught a flicker in her eyes before she turned them down to her notebook, and I realised that this was as close to an attempt at real conversation as I had made in all my visits to her office.

"It might help us if we could find out, don't you think?" Her pen was busy again, with its painful scratching. "I wonder what would happen if you took George back to the beginning, to that first time he disappeared, went away, died if you like. You remember he was on the bus, and the first thing that bothered him was that Alice would be angry with him for being late, that she would be worried." She drew my earlier manuscript from the folder on her desk. "You say here that Alice would be worrying if George didn't get off the bus as usual at the top of the road. If he really thought he was dead wouldn't this have been a minor concern?"

I wanted to fill in the pause with disagreement, but no words would come without pen and paper to buffer me from the pain of direct communication. Ann's worrying, and her disapproval, had never been a minor concern for me, especially since she always did the worrying for both of us, making guilt take the place of worry in me. No doubt Dr. Gagnon would make something of that too: sex and now guilt, I was becoming a psychiatrist's dream; I almost smiled—a strange experience, I discovered—but the only response I could manage was to shake my head and look away. I sat saying nothing while the agony of her pen grew in my ears, fingernails scraping down a dirty window pane. The rest of the hour was filled with flickering silence.

✧

The bus must just have been passing Pennyfuir cemetery that first time, because George remembered thinking before he found himself missing that he was glad the bus driver was responsible for passing the big transport truck, just there, and not himself. The sharp Z-bend on the narrow road was a notorious hazard, and he had always slowed down his old Morris Minor almost to walking pace driving round it. There had been many accidents on that bend, one of them involving two friends, an elderly couple, Cameron Morrison and his wife, who were killed by a drunk driver on their way to church one wet Sunday night. Always after that, Alice was terrified of driving, which had been why they had sold the car and only travelled by bus. Now it came back to him—George had been thinking about the Morrisons and their accident as they got to Pennyfuir; how strange it was to be killed just outside the walls of the cemetery where they were buried. He and Alice often visited their grave on Sunday walks and replaced the wildflowers in the vase the family had placed there, then neglected. It was a beautiful cemetery, looking over a narrow sound to a low island, with larger mountainous islands beyond; if people who died so violently could ever be at peace, it would be here, they often said. The soft wind in the trees carried with it echoes of their gentle, highland voices.

✧

She took longer than usual to read my script, though it was shorter than most, and took many notes as she did so. Half-way through, she opened the file folder and compared the script with one of my previous ones. As she put them both down she didn't say, "Very interesting," but it was what she meant. There was a glint in her eyes that I had not seen before. "You said in that earlier script that most teachers in Scotland at the time George was living there didn't have cars—I thought you were implying then that he didn't have one either, and was forced to use the bus. Now you tell me that he did have a car, but gave it up when their friends were killed. I find that an interesting inconsistency, I think not there by accident. We don't believe much in accidents, we psychiatrists, you know. Most things happen because someone wanted them to. Most clues are planted because someone wants us to find them. Even road accidents have causes that we may know nothing about."

Inside I protested. Who could have wanted Dougie and Morag McIntyre dead, mangled on their way to church, as kind and friendly a couple as anyone could have had for friends. They had practically adopted us, when we settled in the village, and treated the girls almost as their own grandchildren. What else was that if it wasn't an accident? They hadn't wanted to die, that drunk hadn't wanted to kill them. I hadn't wanted to sell the car to give in to Ann's terror, to my own; but that wasn't it. I did want to speak, to explain. I couldn't. "I don't think that's true" was all I could say.

"That there are no accidents? That George didn't own a car? That that's what you were implying? What isn't true, Mr. Walker?" There was no excitement in her soft voice, but I sensed an electric control that was not usually there. She stood up, and walked round the desk to stand over my chair. "I want you to write down your answer before you leave today. What do you think is not true in what I said?" She gave me some paper and a pencil, then left the room.

✧

"Hi, George," Kirsty MacCallum's voice danced into the car when he opened the door for her at the Girls' Hostel, where she was resident mistress. "What a waste of a Sunday—another of Ewen's informal staff meetings. Thank God for his Islay malt and Mary's trout salad." She was as old as he was, but there was a bubbling vitality in her, a kind of sports-mistress' sexual healthiness that made her seem young and exciting. The girls in the hostel, who lodged there because their homes were in the remoter islands, adored her.

In school George and Kirsty were allies in most of the in-fighting about exam policies and curriculum, and for the last year they had served together as the school's representatives on the National Educational Institute. It was on their weekends together in Edinburgh that they had become lovers; they were very discreet about it at home, and were sure no-one suspected. Afternoons together like this that they could steal in apparent innocence were rare, and George took a round-about route to Ewen's that enabled them to park the car for a frantic session of love making in an abandoned slate quarry before tidying up for the meeting.

It was too late when they left Ewen's to dare a repetition of the afternoon, though they were both in a pretty flushed state by then—a couple of nips each of Ewen's Special Laphraoig, and the wine with the sea trout, had been more than enough. On the drive home along the Pennyfuir road, Kirsty had snuggled as close to him as the uncomfortable divided seats would allow—she was always very affectionate even after a very little to drink. When he protested that someone in a passing car might see them, she just giggled.

As they climbed up the winding road out of town, just at the crest of the hill, a small grey car drew out of a side street right in front of them, making George brake and swerve. Then, maddeningly, it slowed down as though challenging them to overtake. Kirsty stroked her open hand up his inner thigh. "Come on George, pass him, pass him. He wants a race." There was a charged excitement in her voice that stirred him. The old car did not have much power, but George put the pedal to the floor and squeezed past.

He remembered the scornful face of the driver inside, and the three passengers, all young men, waving beer bottles at him and laughing. One of them made an obscene gesture to Kirsty, curling his fingers and thumb round the neck of his bottle and pumping them up and down. No sooner had he passed than the other driver speeded up again and rode for a while almost on his back bumper, forcing George to accelerate so he could keep clear. Just before the dangerous bend he drew away from them, but hit the corner going too fast and slid sideways on the wet road. The rest was a blur only. Another car, coming towards him, swerved to miss him and lost control; in a grinding, crashing, horrifying explosion it smashed head on into the drunks as they screeched round the corner on the wrong side. George pulled his car up as soon as he could, and both he and Kirsty ran back to the tangled mess. George cried out in agony when he got close enough to recognize the overturned car through the flames. "It's the Morrisons, oh God, it's the Morrisons." He seized the handle on the passenger side of the little red Ford, but the heat drove him back, although not before he caught a glimpse of fingers grasping hopelessly at the inside of the glass, and for the minutest fragment of time, Kate Morrison's face, recognition on it contorted into agony, before it was swallowed by the flames.

The car was Cameron Morrison's pride and joy that only he drove. On a Sunday evening at that time they would have been going to church in town. When he realised that he couldn't get near the car for the heat, George tried to comfort Kirsty, lying to her with the hope that the Morrisons had died instantly from the impact; he tried to forget and didn't tell her about the look of recognition on Kate's face or the clawing fingernails. Finally a whooshing upsurge of light and heat physically blew them back as it totally consumed the rest of the car. Four bodies from the grey car were strewn, lifeless, across the road among shards of broken glass; an undamaged beer bottle, rolled clear from the wreck, lay spinning on the crest of the road. "We mustn't be found here, Kirsty," George had said, holding her sobbing body, "and there's nothing we can do anyway. We'd better get home." He drove her back to the hostel in silence, then went home himself.

Later that night, the Morrisons' oldest boy Calum, his tall young body shaken and somehow diminished, came to tell the Robertsons that his parents had both been killed in a road accident.

"It was that tinker Dougie McQuoich who was driving

the other car, drunk as usual. He's still in a coma in the Glengarten, and all the rest dead. If there's any justice he'll die slowly."

Alice was, of course, crushed by his news, but she tried to comfort Calum as best she could, in spite of her own distress. "You and Archie will have your tea with us tomorrow night, and I'll be up to look after the house. We'll all get through this together, Calum." And she took his sobbing frame in her arms and rocked him like a child.

George kept his panic to himself, for what if the McQuoich boy recognized them, what if he recovered? When Ewan MacDonald said the next day in school that George and Kirsty were lucky, and that they must just have missed the terrible crash, they could only agree. But they knew that whatever there had been between them was over for good; they met only once or twice after that, outside school, and never made love together again.

Dougie McQuoich was never brought to trial, for he died without regaining consciousness after a week in the hospital. That July, Kirsty accepted a position with a Ministry of Defence School in Singapore, and in August the Robertsons moved to Canada.

✧

I was standing by the window when Dr. Gagnon came back into the room, looking out past the gaunt maples towards the great iron gate at the hospital entrance. The finished script was on her desk, the pencil, which I had snapped in two, beside it. As she was reading it, I spoke more freely than I had done for months, looking not at her but at the waving, gesturing trees. "I don't think I'm going to need you much longer," I said. "They can call my wife, and tell her to pick me up soon. We have a lot to discuss. I think you've helped me all you can." Lifting her eyes from the paper, she nodded. When I held out my hand, instead of shaking it, she turned it over to look at my finger tips. "No scars?" she asked. I looked into her eyes for the first time since becoming her patient. "No, no scars, not there," and I turned to leave. She picked up the folder and handed it to me at the door. "Perhaps your wife might like to read this," she said. For a moment I held it in my hand, then gave it back to her.

"No, I have a story of my own to tell her. This belongs to someone we don't know."

The BEAUTY of HOLINESS

✧

"Why'd Grandma keep all these books, Dad?" Faith's straining voice echoed hollowly from deep inside the sturdy cardboard packing case. For an eleven-year-old she was not very tall and found it hard to reach right to the bottom. She emerged clutching a book in each hand, brushing a strand of long brown hair from her face with her forearm.

"Oh, I don't know, she was never much one for throwing anything away. Always thought it might come in useful some day. She always used to say 'Keep something for ten years, then throw it away, and next day you'll find you need it.' Maybe she thought my children would like them."

Faith smiled, as much in amusement at the ridiculous suggestion that she would ever want these old things as at my impression of my mother's Scottish voice. Right enough, there was not much chance that she or her younger sister would be interested in *The Boys' Own Annual* for nineteen-forty-eight, or *Cairncross' Introduction to Algebra* (O.U.P., 1938 edition).

She was like my mother in many ways, with her wistful, oversized hazel eyes and squarish nose; she had the same quick temper, too, and ready laugh, and was even left-handed as her grandmother had been. They had never known each other because my mother had been crippled by a stroke two years before Faith was born, and had lived in a nursing home until her recent death.

"Look at this one—it's hardly ever been opened, looks like. Hey, Dad, it was a prize you won. See—" and she pointed to a certificate pasted to the end paper, "it says

'Presented to Lawrence Graham for perfect attendance. Netherlaw Parish Church Young Worshippers League, December, nineteen-forty-nine.' " Her tone made the date seem medieval. "Who'd want a book about slaves in Africa—some prize, eh Dad?"

I took the book from her and blew the dust from its yellowing cover. "*Blantyre to Bagamoyo*—David Livingstone frees the slaves"—most of the prize books were of this uplifting nature, I remembered. A turned-down corner on page twenty showed where I had become tired of the inspiring account of the Scottish missionary-explorer's struggles—the rest of the book, as Faith had guessed, had never been opened. What I found even more strange was that, as I took the book in my hand, a residual feeling of shame came over me, so that I could almost feel myself blushing. Surely that wasn't just because I had never finished the book that Jean Munro had picked out specially for me. She was the minister's plain, gentle daughter who organized the Young Worshippers League, and I did remember with some chagrin lying to her after Christmas that year, telling her how interesting the book had been. I had even made up some convincing details drawn not from the book but from a visit my school class had made to Livingstone's Memorial in Blantyre the previous year. He was, after all, something of a local hero, and every kid in the village knew a bit about him, so I was able to impress the gentle spinster with my knowledge, especially since I was her favorite young worshipper. It had been a sore disappointment for her when, the year following, I missed going to church for two Sundays only a few weeks before I would have qualified for the red leather-bound Bible awarded for five years' perfect attendance.

But this shame had an origin more painful than my regret for the minor betrayal of Jean Munro's trust in me, something I wasn't ready yet to share with my daughter. I thought I could make up for it by letting her in on the minor secret. "Yes, you're right, I wasn't very thrilled to get this one, even though every one was very proud of me when I went up to the front of the church to be presented with it. You know, I had to lie to your grandmother and everybody about finishing the book. Did I ever tell you about the Young Worshippers League?" We were not much involved as a family in worship these days, and her puzzlement was understandable. "What was it, some kind of church baseball thing, you know, like Little League?"

"No, no, nothing like that," I smiled. "It was really just a way of getting us kids to attend church regularly. Every Sunday we had our card stamped—a purple stamp for each week, and a gold one if we went for a whole month. At the end of the year those with perfect attendance got a book like this for a prize. It was quite a big thing back in Netherlaw when I was your age."

Faith soon tired of the rest of the stuff my sister had shipped to us when they dismantled my mother's house. There being nothing there that could be considered of much value, her aunt Moira had sent me what she thought my mother would have wanted me to have—the books, an old clock, a few trinkets of jewellery for Faith. Holding these somewhat dubiously, Faith retired to her room, leaving me with the books and my guilty memories.

I picked up the prize again. Through its slight dampness I could sense just the trace of church smell, an odour not of sanctity, but of repression mixed with sticky paint and peppermint.

✧

Granny Walker's faint, sweet, old smell came drifting in with the peppermint. She took me to church before there was a Young Worshippers League, made me sit upright beside her in the tall pew, three from the front on the right-hand side, and not try to look back—that, I came to believe as I listened to more Bible stories, had something to do with Lot's wife, and some terrible goings on in Sodom and Gomorrah, and, having no desire to be turned into a pillar of salt, I rigidly faced front throughout the service. She always called me *Sonny*, not Laurie like every one else, because she thought I should have been named not after my own father but after my mother's father, Alexander Walker, her long dead husband. He was always called Sanny, and Sonny was as near as she could come to that without openly defying my parents. They had the right, of course, to name me what they liked, but she preferred the generic Sonny to my father's name. Her one compromise with my childish lack of interest in the service was to slip me a large peppermint candy from a paper bag in her coat pocket, just before the beginning of the sermon. "Sonny," she would whisper, handing me the sweetie, "Now, don't crunch it." I didn't need this warning, repeated every week, for besides the fact that I would have been mortified to break the holy hush with such a noise, I soon learned that, sucked judiciously, the candy— she called them Imperials—would last through the long sermon, leaving just a tiny piece to be swallowed before the closing hymn.

The church had been redecorated at great expense not long before I started going, and my Granny did not like it much. It was too near what she imagined one of those Catholic places would be like, modest though the ornamentation was. Although the church was half a mile away from the centre of the village, up a steep hill, Granny Walker refused to take the bus to service; it would somehow have been irreligious to go to worship in the same bus our few Catholics took to church in Brideswell, where the nearest R.C. chapel was. So, winter and summer, until she died at ninety-four, she trudged up the hill every Sunday. The church's new coat of heavenly blue paint, picked out in maroon and gold, seemed to her redolent of the luxury and saint-worship that John Knox and the Covenanters had fought against, and she told the minister so, every chance she got.

With my eyes firmly to the front, there was not much for me to do except examine the decoration, for even an innocent diversion like trying to read the hymns at the back of my Bible while the service was going on was like not paying attention to God and therefore frowned upon. Not literally, no, for her eyes would never leave the pulpit as she reached over to close the book, not being too concerned, it seemed to me, if my fingers were caught as she did so. So I committed to memory every swirl and curlicue of the maroon letters set in gold around the arch that sheltered the pulpit, like a rainbow over a ship's prow. "Worship the Lord" it said round one side, and "In the beauty of holiness" round the other. There was an embroidered cloth, too, hanging down from the lectern, which intrigued me. In illuminated letters, done in gold thread it read *I.H.S.*, which my Granny said meant "In His Service," but which I learned in school later on probably stood for *Iesus Hominum Servator*; since this was Latin, and therefore doctrinally suspect, she wouldn't have admitted to its propriety in the kirk, even if she had known. So I didn't agree with her objections to the decoration, though I hardly dared to admit it, even to myself. One part of it, though, I could have done without, was the paint job on the pews. To make them look like the real oak of the pulpit, they had been painted a nasty shade of yellow, and, as though this wasn't bad enough, they had then been covered with thick varnish. Because the church was dank and damp most of the unheated week, this varnish never dried properly, so that it stuck to the backs of my bare legs during the long periods of sitting. When I rose to sing, my skin made a tiny, rude, ripping noise as it separated from the varnish, a noise which embarrassed me painfully, for I was sure every one else could hear it, too. I tried the most cunning stratagems to avoid this noise, slipped my hands under my knees to ease them free as the hymn or psalm was being announced, tried to keep my short pant legs underneath to keep my skin from contact with the tackiness, but none of this was easy, sitting next to Granny Walker, for whom fidgeting was worse even than crunching.

My parents and Moira, who was nine years older than I, had stopped going to church just before I was born, something to do with a quarrel about a drama club my father and mother had started. Their rehearsals in the church hall had offended some of the session, even though it was not a church club, and letting Theresa Fallon, a Catholic, play the lead in *Juno and The Paycock* had led to an awful uproar, with special meetings of the Board of Managers to discuss how it could all be stopped. I had to piece all this together for myself over the years, because it was never mentioned in the house in my hearing. But there was a row in the family as well, since Granny Walker, as you might expect, sided with the Board, and thought my father was, as usual, just being a trouble maker. Neither my father nor my mother ever set foot inside the church again until long after my grandmother died, though they did allow her to take me to the service each Sunday morning. I suppose I was their token of support for religion, a sign that they were still believers even if the church made it impossible for them to practise their beliefs. There were times when I felt like Isaac, being offered up as a sacrifice to Granny's righteousness; the Old Testament story of the trial of Abraham's trust in God had a strong attraction for me, mostly because I could not see my own gentle father ever being party to such a cruel trick, no matter what voice from on high told him to. The Kirk was much taken by Old Testament symbolism. Its official badge was Moses' burning bush; the verse from *Exodus*, "and behold the bush burned with fire, and the bush was not consumed" was a kind of a slogan for the faithful. It just made me think of my Granny.

When Jean Munro started the Young Worshippers League, my parents persuaded Granny to let me sit up in the gallery with the other seven or so regular attenders, under Jean's gentler tutelage. "It'll give him something to work for, mother," my mother had said, "and he'll feel better sitting with the other young ones." In spite of her misgivings that I would just squirm and fidget, once out of her reach, and that people shouldn't need rewards for going to the Lord's House—though maybe it was what some people needed—Granny agreed that I should be allowed to enroll. Of course, I still had to walk with her up the hill every Sunday, meeting her at precisely ten-fifteen outside her gate.

After that I wouldn't have missed service for the world. The place took on a new perspective entirely from up in the gallery. When you've seen the thinning patches on people's heads, and watched august members of the Kirk Session dozing off during the sermon, and watched others furtively reading the *Song of Solomon* when the rest of the congregation were devoutly following along in the *Acts of the Apostles*, somehow it all assumes different proportions. Jean Munro was a tolerant guide, and objected only when one of her less disciplined Young Worshippers made to drop a candy wrapper into a hat below. She was tall, slightly round-shouldered, with limp brown hair, and her eyes always seemed to me to be sad, even surrounded by her gentle smile. Her father had been a widower for years and she looked after the manse, and did the work that her mother would have been expected to do if she were alive, as well as keeping on her own job as the book-keeper for the local jam works. I can only suppose that she never considered marriage, or that no-one had ever considered marriage with her. When I was twelve or so, I loved her and would have done almost anything to please her, and I think now looking back she knew this, and was grateful.

From up in the gallery, too, I could really enjoy the communion services that were held every quarter. Downstairs, with Granny, they had been even more of a trial than the usual services, because she took them with such deadly seriousness. Members of the church, "Communicant Members" they were called, weren't supposed to miss more than one communion service a year without a good excuse—the elders had long since given up visiting our house to question my parents for their non-attendance—so the ritual of the service had an almost defiant feeling to it, with people there in the church who hadn't been since the last communion. It gave Granny Walker an opportunity to be even more righteous than usual, and that translated into more rigid rules of behaviour for me. She wouldn't even give me the customary peppermint on those Sundays, because, I suppose, it would have seemed like sacrilege to mix such frivolity with the holy sacrament. Upstairs, though, I found the service fascinating. On those Sundays the elders took the place of the usually pitiful choir in the two rows of seats below the pulpit, and Mr. Munro chose hymns that especially suited the male voices—they were all men, of course, in those days, the elders. That was the part I loved most, as their rich, vibrant harmonies resounded up the arch of the roof to where we sat in the gallery. The elders were the village establishment, even more than the minister himself, who was never allowed to forget that he was just an employee, though they wouldn't have used that word. Leading the base section was Dan Robertson, the tailor, called Needle Dan to differentiate him from the other Dan Robertson, who was the manager of the Co-Op. At his side was Dr. Gardiner, known behind his back as Peel Wull because of his reputation for prescribing pills—called peels—for any ailment brought to his surgery, even, it was rumoured, a sore toe. The tenors were led by the most famous person in the village, Mr. Muircroft, whose name was in the Sunday papers every week as the referee of one of the Saturday's First Division matches: J.D. Muircroft, Netherlaw, it said, under the report of the game, and since hardly anyone else from the village was ever mentioned in the national press, we were all very proud of him. Dressed in their dark suits—Needle Dan and the doctor always wore morning suits—they would lead the full church in "Ye Gates, Lift up your heads on high," and the whole place reverberated, especially when the basses asked, "And who of glory is the king?" and the tenors answered, "Even that same Lord, that great in might and strong in battle is." That really thrilled me, and I raised my boy soprano with great gusto in the parts the congregation sang. Downstairs with Granny, I hadn't dared sing with such fervour and enthusiasm, because she would have thought that was just showing off, and unseemly in the Lord's praise. She wasn't one much for the making of joyful noises, not when you were my age, at any rate. But up in the gallery I could sing, joyful and unconfined, like a blackbird in the rafters. I still remember most of the words to the hymns and metrical psalms that we sang in those services. I built up quite a reputation for piety and faithfulness, those first years of the Y.W.L., and there were even suggestions by some of Granny's friends that I should go in for the ministry when I grew up. Each December for four years I was given the top prize, for I not only attended every Sunday, and even persuaded my parents to take me to church when we were on holiday, but I also came top when it came to memorizing verses of scripture for recitation at the annual prize-giving, beating out even Letty MacMillan, who was generally regarded as the village genius and later became a professor of Classics at Glasgow University. My parents would have come to see me receiving my awards, but their pride in me was not enough to overcome either their stubbornness, or their reluctance to let Granny Walker crow over them for only coming to church for the wrong reasons. And I didn't really mind, for I had Jean's transparent delight in my accomplishments to keep me going.

The day I was to receive the David Livingstone book—I didn't know this was the prize, only that it was to be a special book for my fourth year of perfect attendance—I wasn't supposed to be in Church at all. There had been a family crisis, for my sister Moira had admitted the Tuesday before, when challenged by my mother who had an infallible eye for such things, that she was two months pregnant. There were many sad-faced recriminations, and one especially nasty meeting with her boyfriend Ian and his widowed mother that I overheard sitting unnoticed at the top of the stairs. Being too young, I was supposed to be kept in the dark about these shameful goings-on, and had been sent to bed. "It's not my boy's fault if some wee hoor sets herself out to trap him," Mrs. Brand had said in her nasal, sing-song, and Ian to his credit had told her to shut her foul mouth; then she had cried bitterly and my mother had made her a cup of tea. Moira and Ian went out for a walk, and when they came back it was all agreed that they would be married in two weeks. In our small village there were few secrets, and a rushed wedding only ever meant one thing. The church itself became a kind of bulletin board, because the announcement of any wedding in the parish had, by law, to be made for three successive Sundays from the pulpit; but on occasions when a delay would have been unwise, the banns (that was the official name for the announcements) were cried three times on the one Sunday; the minister intoned that some spinster of this parish was to be married to some bachelor, of this or some other parish, on a set day. This was supposed to give anyone knowing of any just cause or impediment why this match was not lawful the opportunity to come forward and make their objections known. On the occasion of unhurried banns the bride-to-be and her fiancé would sit in the service for their kirking, and be congratulated by the congregation after the service for the three Sundays; but on the occasion of a rushed affair, it was customary for members of the shamed family to stay away from church, to save embarrassment. As I say, there were no secrets in our village.

But here was the problem; the Sunday when Moira's banns were to be cried was the day I was to receive my prize. Since no-one else went to church from our family anyway, I was the only one affected—to go or not to go. And Granny Walker—she never missed a Sunday, either, and of course had to be told of Moira's unfortunate condition. Most of this I had to pick up from shameful, pause-filled conversations whispered when I was not supposed to be listening; it had been decided at first that I just wouldn't go that Sunday, and could pick up my prize another time; it was Granny who told them that was not good enough and that she would go with me, shame or no shame. "No need for the whole family," she sniffed, "to be godless heathens. We've never been in more need of Guidance." Somehow it seemed to me that it was my father who was getting the blame for this, not Moira.

For the prize-giving the members of the Y.W.L. were

allowed to sit all together in the front three rows in the side aisle. That way they would be handy to the choir seats where the minister would present the books after the second hymn. Granny Walker, as we were going to the church, asked me if I would like to sit with her for this service, without telling me why; I knew from the look on her face—an unusual, almost pleading look—that it was important to her that she not be alone in her pew that day, and I knew instinctively that it had something to do with the furtive whisperings of the day before. In spite of that I said no, I'd better sit with Miss Munro and the others. I'd just be across the aisle, I said, trying somehow to comfort the pain in her eyes.

I knew I had hurt her, I knew I was letting her down, I knew I was being disloyal, but I couldn't bring myself to give up the pleasure of causing her pain, and I sat with the other Young Worshippers, my excitement for the prize-giving completely outweighed by the misery of waiting for the announcements and the crying of the rushed banns.

"There is a purpose of marriage between Moira Graham, Spinster, of this Parish, and Ian Brand, Bachelor, of the Parish of Wilton—" While the minister, as matter-of-factly as he could, read the banns, I felt shame creeping up my collar and round my ears. Every one in the church was looking at me—this prodigy who had just received such praise from the minister for his diligence in attendance and devotion to the scriptures. He had compounded my shame by remarking that if any young man was marked for the Lord's service, it was Lawrence Graham. I kept my eyes to the floor during the long, repetitive announcement, only once sneaking a glance across the aisle at Granny Walker; she sat, as stiff as the pew back behind her, gazing steadfastly at the pulpit, with no indication that she knew everyone else in the church was looking at her too. I was almost as disturbed by her boldness as by my deep sense that I had betrayed and abandoned her.

After the service I stood with her for a while in the draughty vestibule while the congregation was making its way out of the church. A few of her friends asked to see my prize and admired it, congratulating me and her at the same time. No-one spoke about Moira's wedding; my prize made it possible for them to refer to the family shame just by not mentioning it. "He's such a faithful boy, isn't he, Mrs. Walker? Never misses a Sunday, does he?" They didn't say, "Even this one." They didn't have to. On the way back down the hill, I moved the book into my left hand, and reached, without looking, towards Granny. She stiffened only momentarily, then left her hand in mine.

❖

I peered down into the packing case, looking for a colour, a shape. Beneath some old photo frames I dug up a thick, chunky book in a red slip-case. On the cover, stamped below a layer of sacrilegious dust in blue and gold, there was the motto of the Church of Scotland, a burning bush, with a Latin inscription: *Nec Tamen Consumebatur*. Weighing it in my hand, I remembered; it had been my Granny's richest gift ever.

❖

Jean Munro hadn't been able to award me the Five-Year Perfect Attendance prize that year, because I missed church the last Sunday in November. My father had taken me, with his drama group, to a festival in Aberdeen, and the van he hired broke down late on the Saturday night on the way back in some desolate place on the Fife coast.

They had put us up at the local police station overnight, but by the time we had the van fixed the next morning, it was too late to drive back home in time for me to go to church, even with Ron Grant breaking the speed limit as much as he dared at my father's urgings. Jean would dearly have loved to make an exception for me, she said, but the elders, who donated the money for the prizes, were adamant. Perfect attendance had to be just that, perfect, not nearly perfect, nor just about, but perfect. Like most of their rules for other people, this one was absolute. I won the prize for recitation again that year, but the cherished red Bible eluded me. Since the five-years' attendance had to be consecutive, I would never have another chance. Granny Walker didn't say much about the affair, but her silence when the topic came up was an obvious condemnation of my father; her gift of the Bible that Christmas was as much a reminder of his irresponsibility as a reward for my diligence. It was an unusually expensive gift, for her generosity ran mostly to socks and ties, so I was quite sure that she was saying more than just Happy Christmas. She used gifts as weapons quite a lot, usually against my father, and that made it all the harder for me to explain her tears, years later, at my father's funeral. I remember someone saying that they had never seen her crying before, even when her husband died.

✧

I slipped the book out of its cover, noticing that the red of the Morocco leather had retained most of its richness. The spine was dusty, but the gold leaf on the edge of the pages was still bright, and the cut-out black semi-circles with the abbreviated names of the books of the Bible printed on them for quick reference were still clear and uncurled. On the fly-leaf, in only slightly spidery writing,

Granny had written "To my beloved grandson, Sonny, Christmas, 1950." Printed in capitals that had taken a long time to draw she had added "Worship the Lord in the Beauty of Holiness."

The JOINER

✧

The rough pine board gradually became smooth under the steady strokes of the plane. Jonathan Legassie, the West Coast's expert in Seventeenth-Century literature, joiner of words, not wood, was nonetheless quietly proud of his manual skill; and he enjoyed the sensuous pleasures of his well-equipped basement-workshop—the satisfying balance of the plane under the curved hard-wood handle, the easy slicing of the sharp blade, perfectly set, the tang of fresh shavings. His stubby hands had become soft and indulged, more accustomed to turning brittle, yellowing pages in obscure Jacobean folios than to hefting mallet and chisel; so Jonathan envied the practical men he knew, and found solace for pain at his bench. Even as a student in high school he knew his life was destined to follow other than the rough country roads that would be travelled by his classmates, but years of travel along the more smoothly paved byways of scholarship had never completely cancelled his longing for simpler paths. When his studies confused him, it was the logic of plane and saw that restored his balance.

Releasing the pressure on his bench-vise a little, he ran his thumb appreciatively along the plank's squared edge. It sent a thrill of pleasure up his arm, and his other muscles leapt back across the continent, with some memory of their own, to Tom Buchanan's father's bench in Colton Brook, Carleton County, New Brunswick. They felt the pressure of the big wood-screw vises that Tom had shown him how to use, and through some inexplicable process of retrieval he was seventeen again. He was watching Bucky Buchanan as he bent over a fine piece of oak board by the window of his workshop, the evening sun picking up airborne sawdust as tiny flecks of gold around the joiner's balding head.

He and Tom were friends and rivals all their years in Colton Brook Consolidated—before that, even, at McLure Memorial United Church Sunday School. Outside school, too, they spent all their time together, playing hockey on the snapping crazed ice of the duck pond in the winter, or endless games of catch in the Lions' ball park all summer. He often went with Tom when he had to help out after school and on Saturdays in his father's carpentry shop behind the Irving Gas station.

ALEX BUCHANAN AND SON,
FINE WOODWORK AND JOINERY

it had said in hunter-orange letters on the blue sign outside. The story went that before Tom, the only issue of a late marriage, was a month old the "AND SON" had been proudly added; if you looked closely, you could see where it had been only slightly squeezed into the not-quite-big-enough space at the end of the first line.

Jonathan loved the sight of Bucky's hands as they caressed some especially beautiful piece of birch or maple—the inlay, perhaps, for a table or a buffet, or even a coffin lid; for Bucky was the town's undertaker too, until the funeral parlour in Hartville took away that part of his business. He had a quiet contempt for their caskets, factory-made in the States with flashy metal work and veneer.

"See that trash," he would joke in his gentle Highland voice, "och, I wouldn't be caught dead in one of those." Jonathan smiled to himself, remembering the macabre bent to most of Bucky's humour, and his tales of funerals back on Barra, filled with drunken mourners and less than grieving widows.

He was a careful workman, as canny in his use of wood and tools as he was in his business dealings. Jonathan remembered how he always treated the great table-saw with the utmost respect, pushing the last few inches of a plank through against the singing blade with a piece of scrap wood to keep his hands away from the invisible menace of the whirling teeth. He always examined the wood carefully if it was not new, for any nails hidden in it that could, Jonathan supposed, have ruined the expensive Swedish blade. Once, when the saw was still, Bucky made Jonathan put his fingertips on the edge of the blade to feel just how sharp it was, and he never forgot the shiver that tingled right to his spine as he felt the prick of the jagged steel.

In a book-lined corner at the other side of the basement workshop, Jonathan's fingertips felt for the letters on the keyboard of his personal computer. He was having trouble with an article for the department's *Journal of Criticism* on an aspect of Jacobean drama. Though he had promised Judith, the editor, he would have it ready for the next week, the essay he was trying to shape on mutilation imagery was stubbornly refusing to pattern itself from the confused electricity he had stored in the machine. The scenes from Ford's most savage play were sharply chiseled on his mind—young, handsome Giovanni with his sister Annabella's heart on his sword, her blood, his blood, mingled with their unborn infant's blood dripping on the terrazzo—the hypocrisy of the cuckolding cuckold Soranzo—the lascivious innocence of the two sibling lovers—the vicious, sanctimonious Cardinal—the distraught father—all danced in wierd hieroglyphics, and refused to come to any but the most rudimentary electronic coherence. He tried to begin again.

> *Ford depicts a society that is much more corrupt than any that Hamlet could possibly have imagined. Indeed it seems inconceivable that even Shakespeare's darkest vision could have produced the moral horrors of* 'Tis Pity She's A Whore. *Morality, religion, family life—all are shown distorted and mangled, in language and imagery which does not merely display, but in a crude kind of physical punning, exemplifies mutilation.*

It still didn't feel right; almost without conscious mental guidance his fingers strayed over the keys, tapping into horrors in his own memory, blending them with the machine's. In the story which he started to shape, he found himself reshaping events of his own past to make them fit Ford's world of horrors, changing names and characters until they had a new reality in the pulsating green symbols on the screen. It was as though the computer's soft sighing was an extension of his own breath.

Tom (if he was based on Giovanni from the play, *Ian* would be the Scottish form of that, wouldn't it?) had been growing more and more like his father in so many ways. In his behaviour there was the same kind of solid conservatism—in his way of speaking even, there were traces of the softness of his father's dialect. In build, too, they were both short and solid, as though drawn up with a set-square, marked out with an awl and carved into shape with a broad chisel. What was left of Bucky's (a modern Ford would have called the father something like *Florrie*) hair was nearly white, but under certain lighting you could still see traces, around the ears especially, of the auburn that flashed in Ian's otherwise dark, tight, thatch of curls.

Jonathan (what would Ford have called him, the foreign one—*Sören* perhaps?) noticed the resemblance again when he called in at the shop the night of the Sunday School Teachers' Valentine's dance. Standing at the bench, under a bare bulb, Ian looked like a seventeen-year-old Florrie. "Your Dad said you'd be in here. I thought you were going to be ready at half-seven?" He was working at some intricate piece of wood, clamping a tiny piece of metal on its pointed tip. "Yeah, I'm all ready. I just wanted to finish this." He held up a kind of locket, a tiny, irregular heart shaped from a piece of birds-eye maple. Taking it in his hand, Sören could see that it must have taken hours to carve and polish. Tiny brass hinges held together its two halves and there was a silver loop at the top through which a fine thong of leather was threaded. "Hey, that's great, Ian. Who's it for—Letty (*Ann Bell* would be about right for her)?" Turning it over he read, neatly inscribed on the back, *I.B.* to *A.B.* "I thought you were supposed to be just like a brother to her—this is a bit personal for that, eh?"

Ann Bell was Ian's partner in the Church badminton league, a pretty, fair-haired girl Sören spent restless nights dreaming about. He had tried to interest her in other sports, physical too, in their own way, but she had never shown any interest, nor given him any encouragement. Sören had given up, and directed his attention to a succession of other girls; he had never had any hint that Ian thought of her as anything more than a sisterly partner, and the revelation on the locket was a shock.

"Never you mind how personal it is—let's get out of here. Put a stick in the stove, will you, while I tidy up."

Shrugging on his winter coat, Ian ushered Sören out into the frosty night, putting out the light and locking the door as they went. Not for the first time Sören wondered why he bothered locking up; everyone knew that his father Florrie always kept a spare key under an old nail keg beside the door. Any thoughts Ian had about Ann might as well have been under lock and key too, snapped inside the locket, for he wouldn't be drawn on the subject during the short walk to the dance.

In the church hall vestibule, as they were piling coats and gloves on the shelf above the rack, they met Ann. Her face, glowing already from the chilly air, seemed ready to burst when Sören teased her about Ian's gift. "He's a sly devil, you know, making heart-shaped lockets in the dead of night for his Valentine." He pronounced it correctly; Ian, he knew, like all the rest of their friends pronounced it with an "m," as in "time." "You know what they say about those quiet ones, eh?"

"You just be quiet, it's a lovely locket." Turning to Ian, she smiled shyly. "Thanks, did you really make this yourself? It's so delicate. I can hardly believe. . . . "

"That a clumsy badminton player like him could make such a thing? Maybe if you ask us nicely we'll take you to the workshop after to show you how he did it—how about it, Ian, that be all right?"

Ian glowered at him. "What would she want to see that messy place for? Girls aren't interested in woodwork."

"What makes you think that? I've always wondered what your Dad's shop looked like inside. Would you really show it to me?" Ann showed in her look that Sören was not included in the "you"; but he chose to ignore the implication.

"Sure we will, right after the last dance. Your Dad wouldn't mind, would he?"

And of course Ian had to agree. Sören danced with more abandon that night than he had ever done, jiving in the current wild local style with all of the girls in their group in turn. Several trips out to the kitchen with Bernie Baker helped relieve his inhibitions too, for Bernie—fat, ugly, smelly Bernie—was only too pleased to share furtive swigs from his bottle of Captain Morgan with anyone who could stand him. When Sören danced with Ann—since she and Ian were not yet a recognized couple, he was free to ask her, and she was not free, by the group code, to refuse—he chose to ignore her cold politeness.

At ten-thirty Podge Stephenson played "The Tennessee Waltz" on his flashy Italian accordion with the romantic flourishes he always reserved for the last dance. Ian and Ann danced together stiffly, too aware of this first public declaration to enjoy the experience much; uncomfortably aware, too, of Sören's nods and winks as he swirled around the floor with Polly Smith, a girl from the next village he sometimes went out with. Since her father had already arrived to take her home, there was no danger Sören would be expected to walk her the three miles to Burton, and then back alone.

After seeing her to her father's high-winged green Pontiac, he went back into the hall to find Ian and Ann sitting over by the stage. "Why don't we forget about going to the shop." said Ian. "I've got the money to count up, and the band to pay. . . ." Ian was the treasurer of the Social Fund.

"Hey, no problem, pal—" said Sören, "I'll take Ann to the shop." (Why wouldn't they offer to stay and help him count?) He put a brotherly arm round Ian's shoulders, and smiled at the unsmiling Ann. "I'm quite capable of showing her the ropes myself, you know. How long can it take to finish up here—ten, fifteen minutes? You can come when your onerous duties are satisfactorily completed." He realised with some pride that he could still wind his thick tongue around show-off words, even if Ann did not seem impressed.

"No, Sören, I promised Dad I'd be in by eleven. I'll just go straight home."

George Little

If he had been in a clearer state of mind he would have read the signal in her use of his name; there seemed to be an unbroken rule among them that you didn't address anyone directly by their first name unless you were somehow shocked or angry at them. In some families in the town the kids wouldn't have been able to tell you their mother's or father's first name if you asked them. Names were rarely used in tenderness.

Names—he was quite pleased with this game linking the names in the play with the invented names of the half-remembered, half-created story. But if Jonathan of reality had become *Sören* of created memory, Tom, *Ian* and Letty, *Ann*, how much of the past was he remembering, how much making up? The damned machine made it so easy to change things—you could always pretend that nothing was real or fixed while it was just specks of light on the screen, before the racing printer's stuttering recorded it in tangible words on paper. Jonathan was still a print man, at heart. So the names could change in his story to fit the characters in the play, and he could make the real people in his memory fit Ford's corrupt Jacobean world vision, and it didn't matter because it wasn't fixed, nothing was fixed, and he couldn't be held accountable for it as long as he didn't give it permanence. He wondered, if Ford could have used a word processor, would he have written different plays—if being able to change, by a simple key-shift, the tortured words on his sheets would have tempted him to start over. Or maybe it would just have opened up the possibility of infinitely varied horrors. How would the computer have changed the whole shape of past and therefore current literature? What did Romeo say about his offending name—"Had I it written, I would tear the word?" He couldn't imagine him saying, "Had I it processed, I would delete the word." Having something to tear, even, would be more tangible than pressing a key

76

and obliterating in one stroke an hour's, a week's imaginings, not as a deliberate agonising destruction but as a simple return to the void which had always been there, only decorated by the blips on the screen. He woke up at night sometimes, in panic that somehow a day's writing had been "lost in the electricity," as the computer sophisticates in his department referred to the destruction of material by some glitch; but at other times he would edit and rearrange his sentences interminably rather than put himself to the agony of creating new ones. It saved him from probing into the void.

Inside the workshop Sören fussed around Ann in an officious show of politeness. "Here," he said, "I'll open up the damper on the stove—it'll soon be warm as toast in here. He shouldn't be long." Ann had not said more than a couple of words since they had left the church hall. She had been visibly displeased when Sören had been able to persuade Ian that they should go on ahead to the joinery, and she had probably agreed rather than offend Ian on this special night. Sören could almost smell her distaste for him by the time he unlocked the door with Florrie's hidden key, and showed her in; but instead of repelling him, her distaste seemed rather to offer a barrier to be overcome—hence his exercise in solicitous attention.

"Quite a place this, eh? I bet old Florrie has more tools in here than any other joiner in the province. Brought most of them over with him when he came—did Ian ever tell you any of his Dad's stories about the old country?" He rattled on, still under the stimulation of the rum, to disguise his awareness of Ann's coolness. Better any nonsense than a frosty, unforgiving silence. "Of course all the electric equipment is new. The sanders and stuff, they're all new. That table saw, I heard Florrie telling my Dad it cost him five thousand dollars. Want to see how it works?" He cut off Ann's half-protest, "You better not—"

by throwing the switch to turn on the motor. It was as though he had turned on some current of madness in himself, too, for he was filled with a crazy desire to impress Ann, or to shock her or to scare her—anything to raise a response in her. He raised his voice so she could hear him above the whine of the motor. "You should see old Florrie working this thing—treats it as though it would jump out and bite him. 'Now, Sören, it iss ferry careful you musst alwayce be around the saw—it iss a dangerouss machinery altogether.' " Mocking the joiner, Sören lifted an old plank from the floor and set it on the table with exaggerated care, until its front edge met the whirling blade with a shriek of complaint, whether from the saw or the wood he never knew. "He always pushes the last bit in with this piece of scrap wood," but he turned his head as he said it, to flourish the piece at Ann, and so didn't see the rusted, square-headed nail at the end of the plank when it met the saw. He didn't see it either as it fired like shrapnel to shatter the blue window of Ann's left eye. The reflex covering of the wound with her hand was the only indication he had that anything was wrong until he saw the watery blood oozing down her cheek from underneath fingers trying in vain to hold it in. That was in the instant before she crumpled to the sawdust on the floor; as her lifeless hand left her face he could see the rusted square head of the nail head protruding obscenely from the bleeding centre of where her eye had been.

So many what ifs—infinitely variable in the tedious complexity of the computer's brain. What if Ian were to burst in just then, to push Sören aside and kneel by Ann? In his rage at Sören he tells him that Ann is pregnant, and that if he has put the baby at risk as well as Ann he would kill him. They go to fetch Doctor Galbraith, but he is out on another call, and before they can drive her to the hospital in town, she has developed blood poisoning; in a few days she is dead. Or maybe it is Florrie, surprised to see lights in his shop windows at that hour, who finds them. He pulls the nail out with a pair of fine-nosed pliers and the blood gushes out, soaking his plaid workshirt; he sends Sören for the doctor, but, by the time the doctor comes, Ann's cheek is already red and swollen. She never emerges from the coma. When Ian comes he rushes at Sören with a chisel raised to kill him; grappling to part them Florrie is forced across the still whirling saw blade—

And none of that really happened at all, none of it. Letty had more sense than to go anywhere with Jonathan that night, or to take Tom seriously either, for that matter. She went away to work in a government office in Fredericton after they graduated, married a vet and moved to Halifax. Tom stayed in Colton Brook; when Bucky died and was buried in the coffin he had made for himself years before, Tom took over the business. Jonathan had been away in Vancouver doing post-graduate work when it happened and didn't make it home for the funeral; but in a drunk confession one night long afterwards Tom told Jonathan how he had found his father. "His arm was nearly off at the shoulder and the saw was spraying his blood all over the shop. Do you know what slippy stuff blood is—I fell in it twice before I could get to the switch. All his tools were coated in it, like someone had done a bad job of painting. When old Galbraith examined him he said my father would have been dead from the heart attack before the blade drew him in. But you should have seen his face, Jon, the sheer agony on it wasn't from a heart attack."

They both got very drunk that night on the secret supply of Scotch that Tom had taken to keeping hidden in the lumber loft where his wife couldn't find it. Tom promised tearfully that he wouldn't let Jonathan be buried in a Hartville casket; he would make one each for them with the same tools his father had used, long before they were needed.

Tom's life just became unravelled after that as the drink took him over; business fell off until the only customers were townsfolk who came out of pity or loyalty, and who didn't mind waiting weeks for simple jobs that were badly done when they eventually got them. On visits home, Jonathan had tried to straighten him out; he was much admired in the town for his efforts, not least by Tom's wife—she had been Polly Smith before they were married —who came to treat Jonathan as a father confessor-cum-marriage counsellor-cum-financial adviser, and made often impossible demands on him for help, asking advice about the health problems that even her doctor had been unable to help her with, and expecting him to have instant solutions to all her ills. She had taken to calling him when Tom wouldn't get up in the morning, not caring, it seemed, that it was the middle of the night in Victoria. When the phone had rung last night at three o'clock he was mad at first. "Polly, you've got to stop this," he had started to say before something in the raised pitch and desperate tone of her voice warned him to ask, "What's wrong?" Through her breaking voice he heard "It's Tom. He woke up in the middle of the night with this pain in his head. The new doctor sent an ambulance right away, and I went with him. Jon—Tom's dead, he was only in there an hour. They came and told me, a blood clot on his brain, they said, they never even got him on to the table. You know what Jon, he was saying just last week, he was going to start making his own coffin just like his Father did. How can I bury him in one of those factory-made things?" She had babbled on until Jonathan promised he would catch the first flight to Fredericton on Monday—it was Sunday she phoned.

He went back to his bench, leaving the computer stored

with its images of blood, ancient and modern. Taking the shelf from the vise, he leaned it against the wall and started to plane another plank, already cut to size. "He always said no Buchanan would ever be buried in one of those American caskets," Polly had said, "but he never got around to making his own, like his Dad did. You know he hasn't been as well organized these last years as he used to be." As his plane shaved the wood to smoothness, there was a keen agony in its cutting. Even if there was enough time he would not have the skills to make Tom's coffin, but something in the substance of the wood, in its grain and weight and shape, linked him to the death, almost as though it were asking him again, "What if?"

The tree had once been real, the wood was real, the shaping edge of the plane blade was real. Bucky's and Tom's deaths were real, his pain was real. No process, whether in scratched-out and overwritten manuscript, or in corrected print, or in electronic symbols as insubstantial as breath could ever change that.

MAROONED

✧

It is June, 1935. An old woman lies in bed in a white-washed room in the lunatic asylum of Saint Mary of Bethlehem in a fishing town on the Fundy coast of Nova Scotia; shrunken now, thin and gaunt, she has been a tall, robust, big-boned woman. She sits up in bed, rocking back and forward, with a small bundle of white bedclothing clasped to her dried-up breast. From time to time she croons to it, as though it were a baby; but there is nothing in the bundle except a blanket.

She never has any visitors, for she has no children and she has outlived three husbands. Her toothless mouth moves in a rhythmic chewing, as though her old hard gums were at work on some tough unpalatable meat, and in pauses in her storytelling, the skin of her cheeks folds and unfolds in incessant rumination. But her eyes, which are turned to the harbour outside the window, are clear; though their colour has faded, they have been a deep aquamarine. Most days they are stormy and troubled, but today as for the past week a calm sits in them, the calm of a turning tide in a sheltered bay. If you could have approached the bed close enough to look deep into their placid blue you would have seen reflected there other far distant seas and harbours. For she is not old in the pictures her eyes have recorded and play in her memory. In the prime of her life she has six times sailed round the Horn on sailing ships bound from England to Chile and Australia; she was twice shipwrecked. She has dressed the gangrenous limbs of dying shipmates and attended at crude amputations; to keep alive herself, she has eaten the flesh of the dead.

She once was Sarah Farrington, thirty-five-year-old stewardess on the barque *James W. Elwell*. In the early morning of December 6th, 1872, laden with coal on a voyage round the Horn from Swansea to Valparaiso, it burned and sank; Sarah was rescued, one of only three survivors, after more than ten weeks in an open boat in the frigid waters off Cape Pilar, at the western entrance to the Straits of Magellan. And that is how she thinks of herself. The two husbands and the eventful life she has lived since those terrible days in the open boat might never have happened, for she has no memory of them. No one is left alive now to plumb the full depths of her mystery.

The nun who sits in dazzling white beside her bed knows nothing of her past, but she patiently records what she hears, writing with a gold-nibbed, green fountain pen in a notebook bound in red leather. The old woman sometimes rambles incoherently, but today, as she rocks and stares, she speaks clearly, with the energy and confidence of a woman in the prime of her life, as though telling her story not to the patient nun, but to a reporter on board the ship that rescued her sixty-two years ago. The dialect still has the nasal twang of Sarah Farrington's Liverpool, although she has lived in Nova Scotia for more than half of her long life. The tale she tells has, it seems, been long rehearsed and often repeated, and from time to time as it unfolds, the recording angel makes the sign of the cross, as one believing that it is the devil who speaks the terrible details. It is for proof of this that she has been set the task of sitting for hours on the hard bedside chair, to take down the old woman's lunatic tale.

Sarah is ninety-eight, but today her mind remembers the days on the *Elwell* as though they happened yesterday. She was a big woman then, over six feet tall. There is a yellow, brittle, newspaper clipping from April, 1873, tucked in a Bible in a drawer beside the bed, but the nun, her historian, knows nothing of this report. It is not a Catholic Bible that contains the folded page, so she has never opened it.

◇

On board the *S.S.Tropic*, Wharf 5, Port of Liverpool. April 3, 1873.

Dispatch, by hand, to the Editor, *Liverpool Packet*.

In February of this year this reporter was a passenger on board the White Line Steamer *Tropic* under the command of Captain Parsell, homeward bound from San Francisco to this port. We were off our official route around Cape Horn, the captain having decided to take advantage of favourable wind and weather to steer through Magellan Straits, a course which is considerably shorter and therefore more sparing on coal. On the morning of the fifteenth of that month our lookout spied an open longboat, apparently adrift, off our port bow; on hailing her, we received a feeble response, to the effect that the three on board were survivors of a fire and wreck, and were too weak to row alongside us. The captain ordering our boat lowered, we found in the boat, in an altogether pitiable condition, two men and a woman, who told us they were the only survivors indeed of a crew of fifteen of the Barque, the *James W. Elwell*, Captain John Wren, out of Swansea for Valparaiso. We took them aboard, and offered them what food and medical help we could. Your reporter learned the horrifying details of their story from their captain during the course of our voyage back to England.

The *James W. Elwell*, a barque of 791 tons, was on a

voyage from Swansea laden with coal for Valparaiso, Chile. She caught fire, burned to the water line and sank seventy-two days before the rescue, on the sixth day of December last. The *Elwell* was a ship of the Troop line of Saint John, New Brunswick, one of the Maritime Provinces of Canada. The captain, a part owner in the vessel, is one of the survivors. He is John Wren, a native of the town of Saint Andrews on the Fundy coast of that province; the other man is a young seaman, James Wilson, from Yarmouth, of the neighbouring Canadian province of Nova Scotia. Sarah Farrington, a native of our own great port of Liverpool, is the female survivor. A woman of imposing size and build, ruddy of cheek and reddish-brown of hair, she has arms as muscular as any man's. There is an independence of spirit and cheerfulness in the woman that makes it difficult for one seeing her now to believe the hardships she endured during those ten weeks in the open boat in hostile waters. Mistress Farrington was the stewardess on the ill-fated vessel, and is the widow of the late cook, Edward Farrington, also of this port, who died of an injury before the *Elwell* caught on fire.

The Captain has not words enough to praise the woman. In spite of the supposed weakness of the fair sex, she it was who, by her courage and cheerfulness, kept up the spirits of her fellow sufferers. Although injured herself at the beginning of their ordeal, when she badly sprained a lower limb leaping from the burning ship into the boat, she ignored her own pain in the service of the others. Seeking none of the privileges some might have thought due to her sex, she saw to the equal sharing of the few provisions they had been able to take from their ship before she sank, and often saved them from despair with stories and songs. She is, according to the captain, a genuine heroine, and it is his opinion that, had we not rescued the three in the boat, she would have been the last to succumb.

The city of Liverpool can truly be proud of Sarah Farrington.

✧

At intervals for a week the old woman, all that remains of the robust heroine, has been telling her story, sometimes going over the same experiences again and again, and in her neat copper-plate hand the nun by her bed has recorded it as faithfully as she can, omitting only the obvious repetitions and the occasional lapses into madness in the interest of historical coherence. As befits her devotion to duty and truth, she records even details whose coarseness offends her, though from time to time as she writes, she seeks protection from taint by holding fast with her left hand to the silver crucifix at her belt.

✧

They were the worst days you could ever imagine, those last days; to be cold is one thing, and no hope of ever being warm but to be surrounded by the sight and smell and sounds and touch of death, and no other smell nor sight nor sound nor touch save the salt smell of the sea, and the grey sight of the sea, and the everlasting sound of the sea and the biting cruel touch of the sea, that's another altogether. Most of the men on the boat were a sorry lot, sad weaklings, save only a few. Even the captain had not the sense to provision the boat properly, nor to be sure he had the ship's charts with him before we cast loose. In the latter days he did nothing but talk of dying, and was often in tears over his poor lost wife and child with little thought of anyone else—his own men dying in batches and in ones and twos around him. And of all the crew to be left with, that useless Wilson; never did a day's decent work in his life that one, and to hear him now you'd think he was the saving of us all. Always trying to get more rations than he was due and never willing to do his share of the bailing or the tending of the sick and dying, always dying himself, to hear him moan and whine—I've no time for such pitiful creatures as men are when they fall to being sorry for themselves. Poor George Burt, the carpenter, was the only man left on board worth the name after my poor Eddie died of that knife wound, and after he slipped away from us, Wilson just lay in the bottom of the boat, and wouldn't bail nor trim sail, nor even rise up to the side of the boat to make his water, but did it in the bilges. What a sorry excuse for a man he'll be when he is old enough to be called a man, if he ever is. George Burt, though, when he felt he had suffered enough, he just up and slipped over the side in the dark—by the time we saw what he was about it was too late and he was gone. That was a brave way to go, though some have called suicide the coward's way. He was the last to die.

Not that there was time nor thinking of modesty in such a case; I tried as best as I was able to sit over the stern board to do my business; and after I miscarried the babe Eddie had started within me when I fell from the ship into the boat, the hardships and the cold and the hunger quite stopped up my monthly courses and so saved me another trouble. George Burt tended me then, until the weakness passed, and my swollen ankle healed. The Captain was the funniest Prim Jim you ever saw at that; he would wait until we beached, every morning, to spend the day ashore before he would try to relieve himself in some out of the way corner. The mussels and the other weird shellfish of the region, what there was of them we could find after our ship's provisions ran out, gave us all the terrible stomach cramps and stoppage of the bowels, so his modesty was not offended too often, poor man.

In the boat they were no trouble to me, as men to a woman, I mean. In the early days, we were at very close quarters, with the thirteen of us in the one boat. While there was still some life in them, I would sometimes feel, in the dark, a body pressing against mine; some of the short nights, a hand trying to grope up my skirt or fumble my breasts. But after I boxed ears a few times, and held up to ridicule the ool who would try such tricks they stopped bothering me. The Boston Irishman Lynch was the worst, he seemed like an animal in heat even when everyone around him was shivering in the cold. "Hold me, Sarah darlin'," he would whisper, fumbling in his sodden pants, "where's the harm, sure and us all like to die any minute." The only way was to make him feel foolish before the others. "Listen to this boys," I'd say, "Paddy here wants to people the earth with more Catholics, isn't that always the way, even if he is sickly. I don't think he was ever much of a man even when he was hale, do you?" And they would laugh, and he would slide apart from me on the thwart. I could have turned to the captain for his protection, I suppose, but I trusted my own more. Now George Burt, decent man that he was, I wouldn't have minded comforting him at all, and at the end I used to hold his limp body to mine to give him warmth; but there wasn't another of them worth my attention, in the fashion of a man, you understand. I remember how it was the first time we had to work together, that was when Pope, our first mate, had his leg crushed by a falling spar off the River Plate. George acted as the ship's surgeon as well as its carpenter, and the captain called him below to saw off Pope's leg above the knee. Eddie and I had to hold Pope down on the galley table until he fainted from the pain, for the rum Eddie made him swallow did little to ease it. George used his sharpest saw, and cleaned it well before he set to work on the mangled leg—I've seen real surgeons much less careful with their saw-bones gear. Young McCulloch, the second mate, swooned clean away at the sight and smell of the blood spurting all around the bulkheads and sizzling on the stove, and the rasping of the saw in the bone, and Pope's scream before he fainted. I helped George dip the bleeding stump in the hot pitch tub to cauterize it. We should have known then that this was no common voyage, for after a day the leg was swollen and red with the poisoning, and in four days Pope was dead. He was the first of twelve that we cast on the waves before it was over, Eddie after him from the ship before the fire, and ten from the boat. At the end the captain did not even say the words for the last of them as they slipped into the cold water. It is hard to understand someone like that waster Wilson would be saved while good men like Eddie and George were taken.

Oh, my Eddie! I hardly had time to think of him, with all the trials of the ten weeks adrift. We had just lowered him overboard when the first signs of smoke appeared. I couldn't blame Garlic Freethy for that fight with Eddie, for Eddie sorely tried him all the voyage. He had his own ways, had Eddie, and they took some getting used to. Nobody knows that better than me. Oh but I loved him, with his skinny body and his dandy whiskers, and his cook's pride. And what a lover he was—no wonder none of the others could take his place. And how he loved my body, worshipped it as true to his wedding vows as could ever be. We had only been married two months when we shipped on the *Elwell*. The captain didn't want me on board at all at first. I remember when Eddie took me along to see him at the Liverpool docks.

"I've never sailed with a woman on board, Farrington," says he, in that weird old-fashioned way that every New Brunswick skipper I ever met has, "and I don't intend to start now. They're nothing but trouble. They cannot work

like men; they fall sick too often and need special treat-
ment. Besides they're just plain bad luck, and cause ill
feeling among the men." If he hadn't wanted Eddie as
cook so bad—everyone knew he was the best in England—and if Eddie hadn't told him that I could work as
hard as any two men he had ever come across and was
never sick, and that it was the two of us or nothing, well,
maybe Eddie wouldn't have died screaming in pain, his
arm swollen and black from the blood poisoning, and all
because of a fight with Freethy over garlic. It was Eddie's
pride in his cooking that did it for him in the end; couldn't
stand to hear it slighted. And Freethy with his garlic on
everything he ate, no matter how Eddie cooked it, at last
angered him beyond control. Knife fights are common
enough on all the vessels I've shipped aboard, and the
captain could not be blamed for judging that Freethy acted
in self-defence. I have fought off more than enough randy
seamen with my own knife. And if I had not shipped with
them, I would not have spent seventy-two days starving
and freezing in that leaky open boat and in rocky bays
north of the Horn. Poor Eddie, he could never have sur-
vived those days, without proper food and shelter; he
needed to eat, that man, though you couldn't have told
that from his skin-and-bone body. All his appetites were
strong. Just as well he died before.

I wonder what the captain thinks now of having a
woman on board. He's been telling you people on the
Tropic that he couldn't have done without me, and that
I'm quite a heroine; he will not tell you, though, that I had
twice to hold him back from jumping overboard just the
day before the rescue, and that he nearly lost us all by
panicking when a wave hit us; he steered abeam of it instead of bow on. I had to set him to bailing, and took over
the rudder myself. He has told you as how he was the
one who spied you first; that would have been hard for

him, I think, with his head down in the bilges. When I called out to him that your ship was off our bow, he near fell overboard in excitement, and that shameless Wilson, who had been pretending to be deathly ill for two days, upped as lively as a Mersey cabin boy and cheered and waved.

I don't suppose that he'll tell you, either, of his dread fear of cannibals. He'd be on to us about them all the time, on the boat. "Pagan savages, I've heard tell, these Patagonians," he told us over and over. "They lure ships on to the rocks around the coast, with their fires," and he would shudder and look sick just with the thought. "They roast and eat the poor passengers and crews." He said it like it was the very worst thing he could imagine. And he, rather than risk mixing with such cannibal savages— for he had a terror that they would creep up on us while we slept and carry us off to eat us, if we spent the nights ashore—he would rather starve us all than try to find help from the savages, so great was his fear.

When we lay off in the short nights, we sometimes caught glimpses of fires on the mountain slopes, fires that drew us with their promise of heat and comfort from the biting damp of our clothes; but the captain told us of the savages with their heathenish devil worship, eating the flesh of friend and foe in fiery ritual—he used such words you would have thought he was a preacher. I doubted whether the devil they served was any more cruel than the devils of cold and starvation that lived with us on our miserable boat, or the devil, stronger than both, that spoke to me in the nights of the second month, saying that eating the flesh of our dead was better than dying ourselves of starvation. I suppose they still do not know how I kept up my strength; the captain was so horrified the first time I said, half in jest, that we should eat the flesh of those who died, I never brought it up again; but I did keep my knife by me, and as they died, one at a time, it was easy for me, always by them as their nurse, to cut pieces of their buttocks and their thighs, even their private parts, and hide them from the others when we put them over the side. I forced myself to chew the meat raw along with some seaweed that I picked up on shore during the day, and so kept alive. If the other two would rather starve than eat the flesh of their shipmates that was their concern. Better than me have kept themselves from starving so; there is no time to be squeamish when it is that or dying, with food, however gruesome, to hand. As I ate it, swallowing in spite of my rising gorge, the devil within told me that the dead had no need of it any more, and since our God let the fishes eat all we buried in the deep, he could surely have no objection to letting me have a share. Women are stronger that way than men; the men are the fussy ones when it comes to food, like Eddie and Garlic Freethy and even the captain. I was already stronger in spirit than any of them, and their flesh when they died kept me stronger in body, too. We are stronger in every way when it comes to suffering and staying alive. No man has ever given birth, because everyone knows they could not bear the agony of birthing. I stayed alive because I had to, when they were all dying, or wishing they were dead because the cold was too much for them, or the hunger. None of them had children in them waiting to be born, as I did. I had to live, to bring them to life. If I died they would all die, all those children, die without ever having been born. If God wanted to kill my children, I would rather serve the devil, any devil who would keep me and them alive. As I ate their flesh, I blessed the ones who died, a sacrament to my unborn.

I have my baby now. And I'll hold him to me and sing him songs of the sea; and I'll rock him to sleep as the ship used to rock me, lying tied up in San Francisco or Honolulu; and I'll keep him warm when the icebergs come and the boat drifts in the freezing mist and the winds blow from the South Pole. And most of all I'll keep him safe from the fire, and the dark, and the cannibals. My courses have started again here, on board the *Tropic*, and they are a joy to me, not a curse. For they are a sign that I am alive again, and my baby is alive again, just waiting to be born.

✧

She lays the bundle tenderly beside her and slides down the bed beside it. There, my baby, my Eddie's baby, hush now, she says, hush now and sleep. Singing a tuneless lullaby she pats it softly, in the gentle rhythm of quiet waters. She watches until her eyelids droop over her old blue eyes, and close in dreams of this child she has never had.

The attendant nun completes the last sentence, then delicately puts back on the pen the green top with its shiny gold clip. She blows gently at the page to dry the ink, then closes the book. Rising, she takes the rolled up blanket from the crook of the old woman's arm, shakes it out and folds it over the chair she has been sitting in. She goes to the window and draws the curtains, shutting out the busy harbour, and the noise of the fishermen and the gulls. With one last sign of the cross over the jaws still chewing in sleep, she closes the door gently behind her, leaving the room to the dark and its devils.

The BLUE HARRIS
TWEED COAT

✧

Ａll my life I have been able to make my mother laugh whenever I need to. When I was small it was a skill not to be undervalued, for her temper was as sudden as her mirth, and when I angered her by doing something silly or mischievous or mean, her hand was likely to lash out quickly and viciously at whatever part of me was within reach.

But I developed eyes and ears for the warning signs—a flash of the green eyes behind the glasses, a quick raising of the voice—and learned to duck and adopt a comical pose of terror and submission (and this was many years before I read Lorenz) just long enough for her to pass the absolute peak of fury. Then I would look up at her—even crouching, I didn't have to look up far, for she was only a slight five feet in height—and smile, if I sensed the slightest weakening.

Almost always the pause was enough to call up a bubbling spring of humour. First she would struggle to hold it down, biting her bottom lip and trying to hold onto her frown—and that was a dangerous moment too, for as she realised what I was doing to her—again—her anger struggled to keep the humour down, and sometimes made her swing out in a last attempt to mark her anger on me before she lost it. The best thing then was to dodge smartly and make her miss again, because the mixture of the ridiculous and the futile was sure to win over her temper. Her face would contort for a moment as rage going and laughter coming changed guard on its surface, then her anger would fire its last shot in a frustrated burst, "Oh you, Ronnie," her mouth would bend up at the corners and her eyes would crinkle, and soon we would both be laughing, sometimes gently, sometimes in helpless paroxysms sitting on the floor.

Almost always. Unless, like the time I lied to her about some unjust punishment in school, I made her look foolish. When she stormed up to see Miss Frame, the Grade Five teacher about it, and discovered that I had been given no more than I deserved, and that I had really cheated on the history test, she had to apologize to the teacher in front of my whole class. Her rage that time was silent and died more slowly; it was a day after that before I could make her laugh again, with a comic impression of the look on Miss Frame's face when Mother strode into the classroom.

But now, as she lies with her head on the hospital pillow, her face is distorted by the stroke into a look of permanent, grotesque merriment, as though God has played a trick on her, then fixed her face into a grin so everyone else can see how funny it is. Her ready tongue is useless, so she can now express herself only by tiny moans which I cannot understand. They have no intonation or vocabulary, these puppy-like sounds she makes, though it seems that they are, at a primitive level, a language, one only she knows. She can move her head slightly and close her eyelids, nothing else, and only in their misery can I see that the fixed grin is really a bad joke on all the rest of us too. Her mind is as alert as ever, that much the green eyes tell me, and that is the worst of all.

I try, during my turns to sit with her, spelling off my brother Johnny and his wife Margaret, to amuse her by remembering some of the laughter. "Remember the lovely sky-blue Harris tweed coat? The one with the leather buttons? You told me it would need to be hemmed, but I wanted so bad to show off wearing it home from Simpson's that you let me. Then I fell in the mud puddle and when you caught up with me you were so mad? You threw your handbag at me, and I ducked and it smacked against the front door, then slid down behind me on to the top step, and I couldn't stop giggling, and you laughed too; you had to peel the sodden coat off me and you could hardly do it for laughing?"

It was the sound of the handbag on the door, a ludicrous slap and slither behind me as I crouched on the top step that did it for her that time. Her laughter was shaking her whole slender frame when she grabbed me, so that I could feel the vibrations in my own body—I can feel them again now—and tears ran down her cheeks below her glasses.

Now only a lightening in the cloud over her eyes shows me, in the fixed parody of mirth claiming her face, that she remembers, but it could come from amusement, or pain, or the beginnings of rage. I have no way of knowing.

When I reach out to touch her only slightly greying dark hair, she turns her eyes away from me, towards the big window that looks out on the freezing mist rising from the bay. The twisted mouth drools on the pillow, and the eyes seem to smile when I wipe it dry with a kleenex from a box on the green arborite cabinet by her bed. This resourceful, tough woman has been a widow for thirty years and has brought up three sons by working in a variety of offices and at part-time cleaning jobs to supplement a tiny pension. Her helplessness is an affront, an obscenity.

I never used to have many new clothes—just made-over hand-me-downs from my two older brothers. She always tried to buy good clothes for Barry, the oldest, so that they would last him till he grew out of them, then Johnny until *he* grew out of them, and then me. My trousers were always thick with hems, for I was much smaller than the other two, with four years between Johnny and me. There was a baby girl too, between us, Annie, who died at six weeks. But that hairy blue coat with the leather buttons was special—she had made some extra money cleaning McDavid's Drug Store in town, and that's what she spent it on, a coat for me that she had seen in the shop window, and decided right away I should have. After the accident in the puddle the mud cleaned out as good as new and the coat lasted me for years, first as good, for church and Sunday school, then as I grew, with the hems and cuffs let down, for school. It was still a good coat when the cuffs didn't cover my bony wrists any more, and I had real trouble getting it on and off in the school locker-room. I think she gave it away to a family three down from us, the Rogersons, but I don't remember any of them wearing it.

I had brief moments of remorse that I could manipulate her like that, but mostly as a teenager I used to despise her for being so gullible. Barry and Johnny knew what I was up to—sometimes they would get me, when I was quite small, to ask her for things they knew she would refuse them: money to buy ice cream cones from Chuck Parker, who used to come round every night with his brightly painted cart, ringing his bell so we could hear him streets away. We knew she always said she didn't have money to spare even for nickel ice cream cornets but somehow, when I asked her, she always found enough in her purse for one each.

There was another incident involving a coat that made me feel bad for years. It was a good coat, too, an English-made navy-blue Burberry that she got from a family she cleaned for up on Mount Pleasant Avenue. One day when I was in junior high, I left it on the bus on my way home from a volleyball game; it was a warm April afternoon, and I didn't miss it until the next morning. I hoped it might turn up at the depot, in the lost property office, but it never did. The thing was, I never told her about it until about a week later.

I went to her with my head at a suitably downcast angle. "I don't know how to tell you this, Mum, and I've waited for a week to tell you so I could save you worrying—it might have turned up and then there wouldn't have been any need to tell you at all." I had rehearsed every word, every pause, every earnest glance. "You see, I've lost my good coat on the bus."

How could she be angry, I mean really angry, with such a thoughtful boy, not wanting to worry her. She was angry enough, but responded exactly as I knew she would. I was scolded for being careless: "I know Mum, I don't know what I was thinking about, I was really stupid— " blaming myself first was the best way to blunt her anger—but soon she was saying never mind, we would just make do with my old one until the winter, and then we'd see about getting Barry a new High School Jacket, so Johnny could have his old winter jacket and I could have Johnny's. I thought she had to be real stupid to be taken in like that, but I felt cheap, nevertheless.

The fixed grin on her face, even with her eyes closed, defies me now. Is she raging at us all, lying there? She doesn't have a mirror to look in, for no-one has been cruel enough to hold one up for her, not even my sister-in-law, but I wonder if she feels her twisted face, mocking her. She reminds me of Lazso Nygorny, the most foul-tempered man I ever knew, who used to live on the next block to us in the South End. Lazso—we called him Dopey Ropey behind his back—worked beside me in the lab in the sugar refinery for years, and he had a scar going up from the corner of his mouth that disfigured his face into the sweetest smile you ever saw; he got it when he was a young soldier in the First World War on the Russian front, and he had gone through his life deceiving people into being really pleasant to him, thinking he was smiling at them; then he would shock them with a string of curses in broken English. He was always getting into trouble in bars, on Saturday nights—some guy would offer to buy him a drink and Lazso, smiling sweetly, would growl, "You go fockink off." He was thrown out regularly, until most of the bar-tenders wouldn't even let him in on weekends. I wonder if the stroke has changed my mother, inside, so that the anger I have always been able to divert is now the only emotion she feels. I can't turn it off this time, but I can't turn it on either, and that makes me as powerless as she is.

She has told me often how they didn't think I was going to make it when I was born. Some congestion in my lungs made it hard for me to breathe—that was in days before oxygen tents, and anyway I was born at home in our apartment on Saint Peter's Street, so they had to keep a close watch on me.

"Twice in your first week," she said, "I had to breathe into your mouth and nose when you stopped breathing for yourself, and your whole face went black."

I wonder now if my two-week-old face, looking as though it belonged to a tiny ninety-year-old refugee from Viet-Nam, would have been twisted in my desperate effort to take in air; I wonder if I looked as though I were laughing, as tiny babies sometimes do when they are really in pain from stomach gas. I've seen Margaret and Johnny's kids, their faces lit up by the most beautiful smile just before they belched smelly milk down their Mother's back. Even in infancy it seems our faces are conspiring to mislead the world.

She is so quiet, lying there, that it takes one of her tiny moans to let me know she is awake again, or maybe she was never asleep. I desperately need to make her laugh, to fend off the fury I can sense behind the quiet eyes.

"Remember the party they had at the Legion, and they had a contest for all the kids from five to ten to see who could blow up and burst a balloon quickest?" I sit down beside the bed and rub her lifeless hand in mine. "That rotten Brian Comeau won, and they gave him the prize, a lovely big toy fire-truck. Then you found out he had used a pin, and made them do it over again, and I won this time—was that Mrs. Comeau ever mad when old John McKay announced, 'The winner of the replay is Ronnie Anderson.' "

I remember what she said to Brian's mother. "I never knew a Comeau short of hot air before. I'm not surprised he cheated with the pin, though; he'll likely turn out a little prick, just like his father."

Everybody laughed. "I had never seen you so mad, up till then, and I didn't even know you knew words like that—I thought it was just our Barry that did. But the story got right around town and everybody said these cheating Comeaus had it coming to them. You just recently being a widow likely helped them to be on your side, but nobody liked Mrs. Comeau anyway; she was always so pushy. You and me laughed all the way home that night, though Johnny wouldn't even walk with us, he was so mortified at the fuss, with all his junior high school friends there. I really loved that fire-truck—it had a wind-up motor and a revolving ladder, and doors that opened and a tiny hose you could really unwind. I must have driven you all mad with the siren. It was the best toy I ever had— we could never have afforded to buy one like it. I think Johnny was just jealous."

Brian Comeau is doing seven years in Dorchester now for holding up a gas station in Halifax, and his mother has been in the Provincial for the last twelve years—that's what we used to call the mental hospital, though now it's called Centracare. She went up to the Welfare Department one day, four months after her husband went through the ice in his snow-mobile, smiling politely, with an axe under her coat—she just missed the counsellor's hand with it when she slammed it into the desk top. I wonder if you can tell from her face now if she is laughing or cursing.

I would have been about eight when Dad died—I hardly remember him at all, for he was away in the navy for four of my years. Mostly I remember him for trying to stop her from spoiling me—turning me into a sissy was what he said she was doing when she used to walk to school with my coat if the rain came on during the day. "A bit of rain never hurt anybody," he would say, but she still thought I was delicate. I could never take him in with my tricks, the way I could her, and I sensed he didn't like my sneaky ways much. The more I tried to please him the less he took to me, it seemed. I remember I cried bitterly when he died because I knew then I could never make him love me, not ever. And I never had been able to make him laugh except when he was amused by some silly thing I did, like getting my head stuck in the school railings, and Johnny had to come and push me through, nearly ripping my ears off in his impatience. Johnny never liked me much, either. I suppose, apart from Mother, only Barry did, and he went to Australia when I was fifteen.

I can only guess what the moan means. "Would you like a drink, Mum?" She closes her eyes briefly—it is too weary a movement to be called a blink—so I take it for a no. "Will I get the nurse?" I am still too intimidated and embarrassed by the routine of toileting to attend to it myself—I have convinced myself she would be too—so I always get a nurse when I sense she needs to use the bedpan. She closes her eyes again, and this time she keeps them closed longer; I take it that she is giving up on my obtuseness. I try the only other possibility, for her needs are simple.

"Do you want to know if Johnny's coming today?" Her eyes open. "He should be here any time, him and Margaret. They said three, and it's ten after now." It is almost possible to believe that the smile is real. "They asked the sister if they could bring one of the kids—maybe it'll be today. You'd like that, wouldn't you?" Johnny's boy is called Barry, after his uncle, and he looks like him too, as he is in old school photographs in the album Mum keeps below the television stand. I've noticed that the boy has something of the hold over her that I used to have when I was his age. The other day when I was sitting by her bed a tall, curly-haired young intern came in to say hello, and examine her chart; he looked like Barry must have done when he left twenty-four years ago, and for a minute I caught a new flicker, a spark in her eyes—they looked sadder, too, a moment later. When I told Johnny about it, his face flickered too, as compassion overtook resentment; he has never quite forgiven Barry for his free and easy life, especially when she boasted about how well he is doing in his tourist lodge near Perth. He can never understand why I never married, either—it is as though only he qualifies for the position of head of our family. If he were to apply for the job his résumé would note his wife, his three children, his house in Forest Hills, his big mortgage. He always feels he isn't getting the respect he deserves, especially from Mother. When he speaks about Barry's success he jokes about it in a way she used to call "half Fun and whole Earnest," saying if he is all that successful why doesn't he share it more. Barry sometimes remembers Mother's birthday, and he always sends her money at Christmas, but otherwise we never hear from him; it was only a few years ago that Mum told me he had sent her the money to put me through university, and she made me promise not to tell Johnny. When Johnny phoned him about Mother's stroke, all he asked was "Is there anything I can do?" Since there obviously wasn't, he seems to think he can leave it all to Johnny. It's no more than Johnny expected, and he seems to feel more vindicated than anything else. He uses that same serious jesting tone keeping his own Barry in check when Mum tries to spoil him.

But they arrive by themselves, Margaret dressed up in her best clothes as though for a wedding or a funeral. When Mother's eyes search the room behind them, Margaret says Barry is at a hockey practice.

"We'll make sure he's here tomorrow, Mother," she says, bending to kiss the grin on the pillow. She has that annoying way of speaking, where she always seems to be talking through half a laugh, and you have to look at her to see what's funny. For Margaret, nothing much is really funny. Out in the hallway though, as I am leaving, she tells me that she doesn't want her kids to see Mother like this, and she had told young Barry and his two little sisters the doctors wouldn't allow children in to see her. She'd rather they had only happy memories of their grandmother. I tell her she is probably right.

CIRCLES

✧

Hazel stood by the door and watched Amanda playing. The child's usually bright face was bent over her task, focussed and serious, her short, fair hair reflecting the weak sunlight that bathed her where she sat in the curve of the bay window. It seemed very important to her to arrange her collection of toys (some carved wooden animals, houses from a model African village, five small Scandinavian dolls in bright national costumes, four miniature cars) in a circle around her, and she was applying all her concentration to make it as perfect as possible. Resisting the motherly instinct to move a tiny hippopotamus the half-an-inch that it would have taken to make the circle just right, Hazel went in, kissed Amanda on the top of her sun-warmed head—she did not even look up—and settled easily in her favorite low chair by the bookshelves. She picked up from the glass-topped teak table the book that lay open on it, and, with one more amused glance at her intent daughter, began to read.

Her attention soon drifted from the book, a novel by a militant feminist that Glenna, the office libber—she still called herself that—had recommended. She looked past Amanda through the window to the snow-covered front yard, pleased, in her musing half-awareness that the huge banks of a week ago seemed at last to be shrinking. The cars swishing through run-off water on the busy street outside also contributed to her nice sense of winter's passing.

She loved these days at home, cherished them as jewels of time snatched back from a greedy thief. Her work at the centre was rewarding and exciting and she remembered how she had missed it the year she had stayed home to look after new-born Amanda. But these times with her now, on the half-days she had bargained for, were deeply fulfilling, a warm complement to her professional work with International Development studies and reports.

Amanda moved from her circle, carefully so as not to break it, picked up two favorite books—*Babar* and *Dino the Dinosaur*—and sat back down in her old place. Hazel thought guiltily how she had grudged her the first year. The house had seemed a prison, the demands of the baby an intolerable imposition. She had questioned her own capabilities as a mother, and despised herself for feeling as she did. Jeffrey had tried hard to show understanding, to explain that her feelings were normal; but when he made an effort to persuade her to take some counselling, she had railed at him, calling him insensitive and thoughtless. Wanting only the freedom that she felt, in a kind of panic, was gone forever, and blaming him for its loss, she had refused to let him comfort her tears.

The mailman clattered the letter slot in the front door, and Hazel rose from her chair.

"Let's see if there's a letter from Grandpa," she said, as Amanda looked up.

"Yeah," she breathed, through a sudden smile—letters from Hazel's father were always fun—and ran ahead to the front hallway. Her books were left open in the circle of toys; a blue racing car, which she tipped as she left, balanced momentarily on two wheels before settling back into place.

The colourful letter from Grandpa Bergson stood out from the whites and browns of the others like a burst of early crocuses in the sunny corner of a spring lawn. Amanda recognised the yellow, hand-folded envelope with the bright blue and red Swedish dolls dancing round its border; she gave a yelp of pleasure, snatched the letter from the scattered bundle on the floor and danced with it along the hall to the kitchen table, leaving Hazel to pick up the rest of the mail.

"Come and read what Grampa says, Mummy, is he coming to stay, Oh quick, Mummy, quick, I can't wait."

Hazel smiled as she followed her daughter's chirruping into the cluttered kitchen, cursorily sorting through the other letters. The handwriting on one of them made her stop short, with a minute indrawing of breath. She put it to the bottom of the bundle, not sure whether she wanted to read it or not. But as she perched next to Amanda on the high stool to read her father's letter, her mind was partly on the clear italic script on the letter that lay, not to be opened until privacy, in the pile by her hand.

"Read it again, Mummy, read Grandpa's poetry again—'Mandy, Mandy, sweet as candy'—read it all again."

Hazel smiled and did as she was told, not once, but three times, taking almost as much delight in her father's whimsy as Amanda.

"He'll be coming soon, eh, Mummy?"

Her adoration of Grandpa Bergson was so total, so obvious, that Hazel could only sweep her up and hug her in response.

"Well, he doesn't say, but I expect so, soon. Ottawa's a very far-away place." She held her for a while, gently rocking, and soon the little body relaxed utterly into a sleep that was not disturbed when Hazel carried her to bed in the gnome kingdom of a bedroom that had been her grandfather's gift for her birth.

Back in the kitchen, Hazel poured a mug of only bearably warm coffee, and opened the other letters, mostly bills. She put aside, unopened, three business-like envelopes addressed to Jeffrey, observing a little ritual they had informally developed. Almost all personal letters came to them both from friends, who saw them as one unit—one of the little denials in their marriage of her personhood that Hazel had silently objected to at first. It was as though they saw her now as someone completely different from her pre-marriage self, inseparable from wife and mother. So, when mail arrived for just one of them, she welcomed the restatement of separate existence that it implied. The letter at the bottom was addressed to her as Hazel Bergson Williams; usually only the Credit Union on her cheques still respected her wish to go by her own name—not hyphenated, that would have been too much of an obvious statement—but jointly with Jeffrey's. She was aware of the self-consciousness of what she called her declaration of interdependence, sensed Jeffrey's unacknowledged, faint resentment and partly understood it. She was especially unsure of his real feelings when Alan Davis used the double name on letters like the one she held in her hand.

Alan's gift in letter-writing had always been to make her feel instantly at ease, to make her believe that he was sitting opposite her, talking, instead of in New York. It was hard to comprehend that she had known him for just over a year, for his letters had a familiar openness that she enjoyed with only a few of the friends she had had for much longer. He asked questions about her work with the foreign aid agency, wrote about films he had seen, books he had read; sometimes he wrote about his son and daughter in college, and his wife Flora, who seemed to Hazel to be all that she herself was not—an excellent housekeeper, a born mother. Alan wrote lovingly about the troubles she had, adjusting to the freedom she now had, with the family away from home. Hazel often had thought that she would like to meet Flora, thinking they might be friends, given the chance that geography seemed unlikely to allow. She wished too that Jeffrey could meet Alan, for it seemed inconceivable to her that her husband and this wise, warm friend should be strangers.

Hazel remembered the week-long symposium in Amsterdam that had first brought them together. It had been the first time since Amanda's birth that Hazel had been away from her for more than a few hours, the first time, in fact, that she and Jeffrey had been parted since they were married. The Organization for Aid in Development had chosen her to represent the province at the conference, where plans for what they called "a new thrust in Development Education" were to be worked out, with representatives from agencies in several European countries as well as from all the Canadian provinces and the U.S.A. Alan Davis from the U.N.'s Bureau of Development in New York was the keynote speaker, and in the small group sessions he and Hazel had quickly become allies against the more reactionary delegates. In the brief periods they were allowed for less formal gatherings, they had eaten together, and had even found time for early morning walks along the canals, and through tulip-rich parks. On the last afternoon, before she had to catch her flight from the massive Schipol airport, they had toured the Rembrandts in the Rijksmuseum. Hazel found Alan's frank openness, his complete lack of pretension, a relief from the hale righteousness of many of the other delegates; he seemed to her the most utterly liberated person she had ever met, treating everyone with a pleasant, unforced equality. She had tried to explain to Jeffrey on her return that Alan never made her feel specifically like a wo-man, just like a whole person; it was a paradox that she was not sure Jeffrey could fully grasp, for with him she always felt completely female, not feminine, *female*, sensuous and warm, desired and desiring. Alan's frankness simply made no distinctions for gender; his strength, his gentleness, most of all his humour and laughter were the same for everyone. He made her feel valued for what she knew, for what she did, for who she was.

Or so she had been able to believe after that first conference. Now, as she tapped the unopened envelope with her fingernails, she sensed a tension in her, as though the quick in-breath she had taken when she first saw the letter had never quite been let go. And she knew why.

A month before, the agency had sent Hazel, with two other delegates from the Amsterdam conference, to another weekend of meetings in Toronto, to present a workshop for Canadian agencies. Alan was again resource-leader, but from the time he held her briefly and gave her a neutral kiss, meeting her plane, Hazel had sensed something different in him, some change in their easy relationship. With the others he seemed the same as before, open and free, and with her, too, in company. But when they found time, as in Holland, to be alone together—mostly just walking in the bitter cold through a park near their conference hotel—something had changed. One day Alan had borrowed her toque, while she shielded her ears from the icy wind with her coat hood, and they laughed and joked as before, almost. But it was not quite as before; there were longish silences, not the easy silences of familiar friends, comfortable in their own thoughts and allowing the private thoughts of the other, but awkward, straining pauses when she felt he was on the verge of saying something but couldn't find the words. She found herself laughing too much at the silly jokes Alan used as an avoidance of silence during their time alone, and tried herself to fill in the gaps with patently idle chat about her work. She remembered she had found it impossible to talk about Jeffrey, and Alan had not mentioned Flora.

He made no advances, he did not attempt even to hold her hand on their walks, as she half-expected sometimes he might, not really knowing what her response would be if he did. It was as though some ingredient had been taken from the recipe of their friendship, or added. At any rate, the taste was different. His flight to New York had left an hour before hers to Calgary, and when she saw him turn at the barrier to wave, a look of total misery on his face, his fleeting kiss goodbye, hardly more than a brushing of her lips with his, still burned on her mouth.

She recognised in it the unmistakable, dangerous savour of sexuality. That, she saw, was what was extra, and less. And now his letter ticked against her fingertips like some subversive mailed explosive. She tried to guess its contents, wishing for some emotional detection device that would tell her how exactly they would react to air and light; one that could preferably also foretell her own chemistry's reaction to whatever it contained. Ever since her return she had felt guilty for not telling Jeffrey about the change in Alan; she had really been confused about her own emotions, certain that whatever she told Jeffrey about them would somehow turn into a lie.

She breathed in, then out, then inserted a fingernail under the corner of the envelope and slit it open. As she unfolded the crisp white paper, she saw that the letter was really four, no, five poems, all in Alan's neat script. He had told her before that he had had some poetry published, mostly in obscure little magazines attached to universities, and reading these, she recognized the conciseness of thought and image, the clarity of diction she had heard him display in the addresses he had given in Amsterdam and Toronto. Taken separately, the poems were quite charming, with a kind of tenderness of observation and absence of gush that would, she thought, have gladdened a jaded editor's heart. But together, and in a letter to her, their implication was unmistakable. She found it at the same time threatening and, in spite of herself, exciting.

Obliquely they traced their relationship, Alan and hers, with references to walks along Dutch canals; some allusions to Rembrandt's late self-portraits recalled their morning in the Rijksmuseum. One line asked

> *Of dulling patina how much is age*
> *How much the aging vision;*

another spoke of tulip bulbs

> *whose round perfection*
> *shatters, bursts apart*
> *in flawless, foliated loveliness.*

The last and most explicit spoke of cold walkers in a frozen city, hands crippled by frost, unable to reach out in love to warm each other.

She had read the poems several times before she saw that there was a note still folded in the envelope. In a single paragraph Alan mentioned the national conference next month in Montreal, and wondered if she would be going. Simply that, just a hope to see her there, with no overt invitation, not the slightest suggestion of a change between them. Hazel knew that another reader might think the whole letter was without implication beyond itself, a simple sharing of one friend's work with another, perhaps for criticism or approval. She was angry at Alan for playing this game, for leaving the interpretation of the poems and the letter to her, keeping open for himself the escape hatch of condescending apology for a misunderstanding, should she choose to resent what she thought his intentions were.

She read the poems and the letter again, carefully sifting every image. She felt a growing tension as she came to the paragraph about the conference. Only a week before

she had told Jeffrey that she would be going to Montreal;
she was to present a paper on co-operation between different non-governmental aid programmes; the centre was to
finance the trip for her with funds especially budgeted.
Yet to go now, in the light of this letter's beckoning,
seemed impossible. To show Jeffrey the poems was un-
thinkable too, since she had kept from him the change in
Alan, and to go, not letting him know of her dilemma
would compound the deception. Simply not to go, to
make some excuse and back out, would be letting both
the centre and herself down, for the paper was important
to her, and had already taken up hours of thought and
research. Nor did she wish to admit to herself that her
insecurity was as real as backing out would clearly show
it to be.

Folding the pages she slid them back into the envelope.
She pushed the stool away from the counter and gathered
up the rest of the mail, then carried it rather aimlessly to
the sunlit living room. Her father's bright envelope was
on top of the pile she laid down on the glass table-top—
she knew he would help with her problem if she phoned,
and she would have loved to, for to hear his voice was
always a reassurance in times of trouble. But to ask him
for help, more sure of her trust in him than in Jeffrey for
encouragement, would be a further betrayal. She could
not reach for the phone.

A bright, yellow balloon on the back of his envelope
nudged into her consciousness. Once, when she was little,
he had told her a story about balloons. "Balloons are not
really beautiful, you know; oh, you may think they are,
but what happens when they burst—bang, just like that?
The balloon is still there see, a little piece of rubber here
in my hand, but it is not beautiful anymore. But then I
take another from my pocket," and he did, a deep red one,
"and I blow it up and up," and he did until it was

completely full of air, and glowing in the sunlight, "then tie a knot in the neck," and he did, his big fingers deftly performing the task in a twinkling, "see, now there is the beauty again. Here in my pocket I think you will find another, yes? Just as pretty a red as this one. Now, blow it up only half way. A little more, yes that's enough. Which is more beautiful, mine or yours? Mine, of course. Which is nearer to breaking? Mine too." And he had gone on to tell her about fragile things, china cups and butterflies— only perfect because they are fragile. The beauty, he said, was somewhere in the fragility. Only when it is on the very point of breaking does the balloon fully define its shape and colour; only when it is tested to its limit can it know perfection, when it is just a pinprick away from nothing.

There was a day when she reminded him of that story. He had been speaking about form and rules and patterns as they walked in a park, down by the ocean. It was during his visit that she had first known she was pregnant, and sensing the tension between her and Jeffrey, her father had suggested a walk in the gardens. It was in the miniature Japanese garden that he had spoken about patterns, prompted by the delicate design of the place, a quiet, gentle space set off by a low circular wall from the surrounding lawns. There was a clear brook with grey pebbles and a stylized wooden bridge of unpainted dark wood. A clean path of white stepping stones curved gracefully over patterned gravel and crushed stone.

"What do you suppose is most important to the beauty of this garden?" he had asked her. She had tried different answers—the sounds of the water, the fragrance of the tiny pines, the perfect scale.

"No," he said, "though these are all very important, of course. But what would the garden be without the wall? Its beauty needs something to define it, no? And to restrain it, too. If the wall is not perfect, where is the wholeness of the garden, its integrity?" He showed how the garden's beauty had to push against the wall, testing it and proving it; there must be no emptiness between garden and wall or the garden, receding, would be diminished. If the pressure of the loveliness grew—and he had placed his big palm on the waist-front of her dress in illustration—then all of the wall must expand uniformly in the round to encompass it.

Hazel smiled to herself, remembering the giant hug he had given her. She should have known he would have the answer. Her exploration of her feelings with Alan, she could see now, had been a testing somehow, of freedom and restraints, and for the first time she recognized that it had served, with its tensions, to enlarge her life with Jeffrey and Amanda. She was certain now of that.

Reaching behind the chair, Hazel took a pen and a writing pad from a shelf, and started to write. Yes, she told Alan, she would be in Montreal; she thanked him for the poems, picking out, objectively and critic-like, some images she thought worked best, a few she did not find so effective. Then she told him about balloons, and walls, and Japanese gardens, and how she had come to see and respect the circle of her life. Friends, she said, could be tangents to her circle, could enhance it by their touch, but could never really disrupt it, nor change its perfect shape.

Before she went to wake Amanda, she stooped to clear away the toys, and as she put the last one in the brightly painted box by the window and closed the lid, she thought she could still detect on the carpet the faint outline of an unbroken ring. On her way to her daughter's room, she gently tore Alan's letter and dropped the two neat parts among other papers for recycling in the blue box by the kitchen door.

BROKEN TEETH and FROSTY LEAVES

❖

Crisp leaves filling up the yard on a Thanksgiving weekend, when we always rake them up. (I've hated Thanksgiving ever since that eventful one, and can't stand the smell of baked ham in raisin sauce even yet, fourteen years later. Donnie and I didn't come home for last Sunday's family meal, just to avoid it. But even on Wednesday when we did arrive, the smell of it was still in the house, and I tasted blood in my mouth again.) Our lab Goldie jumping in and out of the piles, making a mess and Dad shouting at her. Aluminum snow shovels—not very efficient at picking up more than a few leaves at a time, but brutally efficient at wrecking a mouth and an adolescence.

The moment that will decide it all. I bend down as Linda brings her shovel up sharply, to shower the leaves on it into the wheelbarrow, and there is a sickening crunching as it hits my mouth, and my teeth's roots pull away from the bone and bend up and out, filling my mouth with pain. Linda trying to cover up her panic blames me as usual—"You never look what you're doing, Angie." She has a point—my balloon always bursts first, and my toys always break before I have had them a day; and Mum blames Dad—"I told you these shovels were no good for leaves, now see what's happened." Goldie runs away and hides under the big fir tree when she senses the spark in the air; just as she does when Dad is trying to help me with my math homework, just before he loses his temper as he always does, and she shoots from under the kitchen table, her claws scratching the shiny cushion floor, to hide in the hall. Dad is concerned about my teeth—maybe he has some premonition of what the dental repairs will cost too, but he turns his worry to anger at Mum's hindsight and shouts at her. "Just shut up, will you; phone the doctor and tell him we'll meet him at the outpatient department." Then he gently pushes my teeth back into place and takes me into the kitchen to wash the blood away. He hugs Linda, too, and I can't figure out why. He tells Mum, as he puts me in the front seat of the car, he is sorry for shouting.

Now we've just come back from Shady Haven Guest House and Restaurant in whose back dining-salon the reception for Linda's wedding was held. Linda and Scott left for Boston on their honeymoon about nine, Scott's parents drove back to Fredericton just after, and everyone else has gone to bed. Donnie doesn't feel right sleeping with me in my parents' house, though they know we live together in Halifax, and likely wouldn't say anything if we had the same bed here; Mum was real funny, asking me if she would make up the bed in the spare room for Donnie, or what, the first time he came to visit; funny and sweet too when I told her Donnie would be more comfortable on his own. Come to think of it, I'm not sure how Dad would have taken it—I got the feeling they hadn't discussed it, because Mum was pretending to be all worldly and modern, as though it was some kind of conspiracy just between her and me; but if it's all right with Mum it's usually all right with him. Donnie's life among our unconventional friends in the Cove Theatre Company hasn't quite wiped out the Sunday school teacher in him, I guess.

Outside the big window of the living room a full moon is lighting up the leaf-strewn yard, and the glinting frost-sparkles are like an outdoor projection of the tiny fireworks I feel going off in the circuitry of my brain. I don't know what I feel about being free from Linda; worse still, I don't know what I should be feeling. My responses to her have always been complex; I hate her and love her, I admire her and despise her, I envy her and pity her, sometimes all at once, sometimes at intervals. Maybe if I just take this quiet time—quiet because every one else in the house is asleep, but quiet especially in her absence, I can work it out.

Dad drove us to the church, Linda and me, in the brown Toyota, cleaned and polished for the occasion. Mum had gone down half an hour earlier than she needed to, just to make sure everything was in place—she likely wanted to give Mr. Arthurs a quick quiz on the service for the sacrament of marriage, in case he might have forgotten it, after sixteen years in Glenbrook United—and to take her own seat up front; Scott was there already with his best man, Andy, doing the groom's job of waiting. Or he was supposed to be, as Dad said before he started singing, turning out of the driveway, a song we all used to sing on our summer camping trips to New England—

> *Mary Ellen at the church turned up*
> *Her Ma turned up and her Pa turned up*
> *Her little sister Gert and her rich old Uncle*
> *Bert*
> *The Parson with his long white coat turned*
> *up—*

and Linda and I joined in, repeating the *turned up*'s at the end of each line. It's a comic song about a groom who takes cold feet just before his wedding, but it was just right to break the tension both Linda and I were feeling. I suppose Dad was too. He sometimes seems to know how to do that, help people through critical times by making them laugh—but other times he just makes things worse. Like the speech he made at the reception poking fun at

Linda and Scott—it would have been more suitable for a celebrity roast, and Linda didn't like it at all. He's got a nice voice though, Dad, and he used to keep us amused with folk songs for hours on those long trips. Linda hugged him, and held on to him with her head on his shoulder for a minute after he stopped in the parking lot at the church, but none of us said anything.

There were only about fifteen guests apart from the families invited to the wedding, but some of the neighbours showed up at the church to wish them well and see the spectacle. Small weddings aren't common in our neighbourhood so I've no doubt there would be talk about it, and speculation whether Linda had to get married. I guess they don't know Linda—nothing as unplanned as a surprise pregnancy would ever be allowed to upset her agenda. I was the one who had to have the abortion my first year in Halifax, before I met Donnie, after Gary, the first great love of my life, took off to act in commercials in Toronto. I've seen him in a couple; he's the guy in the laundromat who has to be shown where to put the fabric softener. Seems suitable somehow.

Donnie and Scott's brother Bob were the ushers. I would have been happier if they had just been married in a Registry Office, for even a small crowd pains me unless I'm on a stage and I have a character to hide behind. I'm not self-conscious, that isn't it at all; if I was just conscious of me there would be no problem, it's the others I'm conscious of—what are they thinking about me, will they laugh if I stumble, will they think my smile is funny. I have always been Linda-conscious, not Angie-conscious, and it has changed the shape of my whole life just as surely as that aluminum blade changed the shape of my mouth.

✧

My capped front teeth felt bigger and more conspicuous than usual when I walked into the church before Linda, trying desperately not to let my bouquet of tiny pink roses shake too much. I had talked Linda out of the step-pause-step kind of progression down the aisle, mainly because I was scared I would fall over in the pause, so I could walk more or less normally, in time to the organ, but I still needed to concentrate enough to prevent me smiling much, and I was glad of that. There hasn't been a day since the accident that I haven't been aware of these teeth. Before I could have them capped when I was fourteen, I went about with two black teeth and didn't smile for two and a half years. Dad has slides and photographs to prove it.

Those weeks of visits to the orthodontist, hours of drilling and packing and root canals just to patch up the mess and more weeks on penicillin to clear up the abscess that formed; there was no point, Dr. Jackson said, trying to cap the teeth right away, while my mouth was still growing. It would be at least two, more likely three years before she could do anything permanent. I could see the real pain stretching ahead of me—I knew, I think, when I cried out "My teeth, my teeth" the instant Linda's shovel hit me that the agony of the broken roots and the needles and the drills would be gone long before the real torment faded, if it ever did—everybody seeing my black teeth and thinking I looked gross.

Being different never seemed to matter to Linda, but all I wanted was to be the same as everyone else. All they wanted me to be was like Linda. Like the third time I was sent to the Principal in Junior High for smoking down by the furnace room, and he said, in his obnoxious, prissy way, "You know you are letting your family down, Angie, why do you do these things? What do you suppose Linda must think of you?" I didn't tell him how little I wanted to care, for my shrugged shoulders were supposed to say it all, but of course I did care—breaking the rules may have made me different from his star student, my sister, but it didn't make me stop wanting to be like her, and for hating them all for wanting me to be like her, too.

Then that dismal year in Flownton, what would have been my Grade Eight year, and Linda's Grade Nine if we had stayed here. What a pain I was, sulking for two weeks after Dad told us he was being transferred to the London office for a year. With the hard time I had given them the year before with my problems in school, they likely thought this would be a good chance to straighten me out. They had this idealised notion of what a year in an English school would do for me, with school uniform and compulsory games—I guess they thought English education hadn't changed since they went to school there. Flownton Comprehensive Secondary School—I hated every minute in it, with its pretensions to "High Academic Standards." All the kids who were going on to do O level and A level exams were put in specially selected classes, and everyone else was left to get by as best they could. That would have suited me fine, but trust Dad to write to the Headmaster over the summer to have Linda and me put in the Academic stream, because "my daughters both plan to go to university in Canada"—he planned that we would was what he should have said; in Grade Seven I didn't have any plans beyond the next cigarette break. So I was put into a class of really bright kids, and made to do Latin and Advanced Mathematics, and I failed miserably; but since I was only there for a year they didn't bother moving me—the teachers chose to ignore me instead, except when it came to field hockey and basketball—even short, ugly kids with black teeth were made to play those, and they bullied me to join in even though I was hopeless at sports, and scared my mouth would be hurt again by some wholesome English girl's swinging stick. Linda was her usual brilliant self, and that didn't make it any easier for me.

God, those English teachers were a pompous lot—always on about the colonies, and making jokes about Indians—Red Indians they called them, to differentiate, I supposed, from the half-dozen or so brown Indians we had in Flownton. I got the feeling they didn't care much for Indians of any shade. The last thing I wanted was the kind of fuss Dad would have made about the slightest hint of racism in the school, so I didn't tell him. They never seemed to make many jokes around Linda—she was a "serious" student, of course, and "excellent at sports" as her report cards said.

I wonder if Miss Arrowsmith still remembers me. She was the only one on the staff that ever tried to speak with me—all the others frequently lectured me, but only she ever seemed to be really interested in what I had to say. After English Composition we used to talk about the stories I wrote—painful stories, full of lonely, suicidal heroines and cruel parents. She told me once she had a birthmark on her nose when she was my age—I could just make out the traces of it underneath her make-up, when she pointed it out—and needed plastic surgery to remove it. She was a tall, slender woman, with straggly fair hair, and outside class I made fun of her gawky walk as much as the others did, but I was grateful for her kindness. She wrote on my report card, "Angela is a sensitive student with considerable ability in composition." She was really a bit of a jerk, but not so much as the others. Or maybe it was just me.

What a dirty bunch those English schoolboys were, the junior ones anyway; the senior boys who seemed to flock around Linda, even though she was just in the third form, were all right; at least they didn't have to wear the dumb school cap. The first and second formers wore the whole school uniform, a kind of bilious green blazer and maroon pants, with that ridiculous maroon-and-green-quartered cap, and they never seemed to change their clothes. Their grey shirts were likely washed once a week, so they all reeked of sweat and dirt; after gym the air in the classroom nearly made me sick. The non-academic girls I mixed with outside class all wore far too much make-up, so I did too, mostly eye shadow and deathly white face-pack; I've got pictures that show me like a raccoon in a wig of long, teased-out hair, my eyes sullen, my mouth a firm line covering my blackened teeth. All the junior girls smoked, so I felt right at home in the filthy lavatories. Mum and Dad could see what was happening, but I just went into hysterics when they tried to talk me into using less paint, or out of wearing the high platform shoes that everyone else was wearing; what did it matter to me that they had bought me brand new shoes before we left home. They were the fashion in New Brunswick, but that was light years away from London. When they wouldn't let me go up to London for the Sex Pistols concert I wouldn't eat for a week—not at official times or with them, though I sneaked out to the chip-shop when I should have been in Science class.

It shouldn't have been a surprise to them that before the first month passed I was speaking like a Londoner; most of the kids spoke a kind of refined Hampshire accent, but the toughs all spoke like cockneys. So these were the ones I copied. Bloody Linda got more and more Canadian, saying "eh" every second phrase, something she wouldn't have been caught dead saying at home. She sewed Maple Leaf badges on her skirts and covered her school books with sleeves advertising Dominion Stores and Canada Dry—she had brought a whole pile of them with her. I didn't cover my books at all except in scrawled, nearly obscene designs representing the best known Rock Bands—as well as the Pistols, the Living Dead were big that year. I guess my parents were lucky that punk fashion didn't really catch on until the year after we were there, or I'd have died my hair green and purple and stuck safety pins in my nostrils. My teeth would have been right in fashion then. As it was, I tried not to mix with anyone who knew I was Canadian, and never told anyone that weird Linda was my sister. The time during the exams when Linda came and spoke to me outside the library before a bunch of my tough friends was really humiliating, especially when she told them she was my sister, like they were all aliens from space or something. They thought she was really strange—and I knew she was. I was glad we had only another couple of weeks left after that before we came back to New Brunswick, so I didn't have to explain her to them much.

Linda is still about an inch taller than me, but in high school, a year ahead of me, she seemed like a goddess with her braided blonde hair down to her waist and her perfect complexion and her big blue eyes. Good at everything too—on the varsity basketball and volleyball teams, gold medallion in swimming, always in the top five in her class. When you look like her you don't want to be the same as all the other kids. Rather than compete with that I just wanted to merge into the background; I was never much good at anything, and some of the teachers never let me forget who my sister was. It got so that for the first year or so in high school when I said my name for the first time in class and the teacher repeated it, "Angela Cameron," I used to say "Yes, I'm Linda's sister" before they could ask, and "No, I'm not as brilliant as she is, so don't build up your hopes."

That year in school after Linda went to Mount A was the happiest I ever spent; I went into drama and got to play Laura in *The Glass Menagerie*. Mr. Hamilton never knew that it was type-casting, for I had the reputation of being a real rebel by that time; I suppose he thought it was drama that turned me around, but it wasn't, it was freedom from Linda. I even did enough work to get into university at the end of the year. It would have been too hard to explain to Mum and Dad why I had to go to a different college than Linda, St. F.X. or UNB, so I went to Mount A, too. In a way it was like challenging the new me to face up to the Linda thing. And I'm glad I did, because, for once, Linda needed me. She couldn't make friends there, and hated the drink-driven social life, so she used to spend most of her time in my room, often crying. That year too, she got really worried she was putting on weight, and was constantly falling on and off diets. She would lose a couple of pounds and be so proud of herself—Mum was always on her back about not eating right, and Linda hated her for it. She would lose heart and put the weight back on again and pig out for a week on pizza and Tim Horton's Double Chocolate doughnuts. I've seen her sitting curled up on my bed eating half a dozen of them in one tearful, guilt-ridden session. If only her teeth hadn't been so perfect I might have started to feel almost like her equal. We both got through our courses without too much trouble, and I talked her into doing props for the drama-club play I had the lead in—Pinter's *Birthday Party*, that was. She wasn't too much taller than me by then, and had got more than slightly overweight—hence her diet binges. But her teeth were perfect and mine were false; though I had stopped thinking she smashed my teeth deliberately, I still wondered, especially after a psychology prof told us he didn't think there was such a thing as an unwilled act, that whatever we do, it's because part of us wants to do it. I still hadn't got used to the capped teeth which seemed only slightly less conspicuous than the blackened originals and I didn't like the way they clicked together if I wasn't careful closing my mouth, with a kind of plasticky sound, not like real teeth. And she had done this to me. And she got the hug.

The only other times I remember Dad driving us without Mum in the car was when he took us out to teach us to drive, the summer I was between high school and Mount A. We had a big, white Dodge station wagon, automatic with power steering, so it was easy to drive. Dad said we should really have been learning on a stick-shift so we would be able to drive any kind of car but the automatic was a lot simpler—we could keep our minds on traffic signs and staying in the right lane and taking corners right. He took us to the Canadian Tire parking lot on Sundays and laid out a course for us with old grocery boxes, then he just left us in the car while he stood and watched. When we could go round the course without hitting the boxes he took us out on to the road and let us drive round the test course. He took us back into the parking lot to practise parallel parking and backing up and emergency stops. I passed my test first time, but Linda failed her parallel parking—that really pissed her off; I think that was the first time she ever failed at anything I passed. That could have been a turning point too, when I think of it. She passed her second time out, but there were a few weeks when I could take the car and she couldn't, unless I was with her. I loved the feeling of driving that car—it was so smooth and responsive, so big, yet it did what I told it. The first time I took it to work, I felt nervous, but only a little; it was too sexual a feeling to be called nervous, though maybe there's not much difference after all. The power of the big eight-cylinder motor seemed somehow to enter me and control me as I was controlling it, possess me as I was possessing it. I don't suppose Dad ever knew what his car did to his little girl. Linda never liked driving as I did; even after she passed her test she would rather let me drive when we were going anywhere together.

She never quite got back her all-star bloom, though she did well in the firm of Financial Analysts she joined out of college. Her weight wasn't a problem anymore and when she met Scott he gave her all the adoration she needed. I didn't think she could ever surprise me again, but even there she had one over me.

Scott drove her down last fall to visit Donnie and me in Halifax. We live on a quiet street in the North End, with rowan trees in a grassy verge along the sidewalk. When we went for a walk, Linda was disgusted by the mangle of leaves and berries lying in the gutter. She said the pits of the rowan berries looked like the bleeding stumps of little broken teeth in such a serious voice that I looked at her quickly, expecting her to say more. But Scott burst in, laughing at the ridiculous image and then changed the subject. I never asked Linda what she meant, mostly because I didn't want her to know how uncomfortable her power over me could still make me feel, but partly too, because it would have brought me up against a dormant raw nerve I didn't want to bring back to painful life.

Now in the quiet of the softly breathing house I want the phone to ring, and I want it to be Linda, calling from Bangor to tell us they have made it that far. I want to tell her I forgive her for the broken teeth and the year in Purgatory and the hug that should have been only mine. And it won't matter if she knows that I am only partly lying.

POLLING LIST

✧

"You always pay most attention to your strongest polls," they told the canvassers at every election school. So what the hell was I doing this sunny Tuesday morning, knocking on doors where they hardly knew we had a name on the ballot, for God's sake, and would never vote for us even if we were the last party with candidates still out of jail. The campaign organizer, brought in from out west to help us win the seat, Karen Stupich, had an idea based on some phone-canvassing that the vote was "soft" here this time, and could be swayed our way, but those of us who had been in the riding longer had our doubts. "Have you ever been down Imperial Drive?" I protested. "There's not a house there would sell for under a quarter of a million—they don't vote N.D.P. down there." There was that smile she had that made me feel I was back in Grade Three suggesting some impossible scheme for raising funds for the school band. "Now Walter, that's not what the phone-canvass says. Just you toddle on down there, and we'll see what you find."

Never mind, what did I know; I was just the candidate. Sometimes I felt like a bridegroom at a wedding, who's only slightly more important than the bouquets or the pew-markers, a necessary but minor piece of the total business. The thought crossed my mind once or twice that I would be better out of the way altogether until the campaign was over, and there would be no danger of me embarrassing her by saying something out of place to Ted Holder at CYNB or to one of the young reporters on the *Clarion*. I had felt her grimacing when I told her, a couple of days after she arrived, that I had agreed to take part in an all-candidates debate on the radio; from then on she did all the arranging of events like that. "The candidate is always the most important canvasser," she told me, with the confidence-building variation of her smile; I supposed it was good to be important for something. So usually I just did what I was told; at the office in the morning she made sure I had a clip-board, a canvass sheet, a poll map, a pencil—to replace the one I lost the day before—filled up my truck with lawn signs and told me she would see me at lunch time; we would meet at the lunch counter in the Best For Less supermarket near the office. That seemed like a fitting place, given the financial straits we were always in. So that was why I was canvassing this poll, when I would have felt much more at home and useful in the run-down apartments just a couple of streets up, along the main road. I could maybe have got a few of them convinced to come out and vote, anyway. Canvassing is always an educational experience, though, no matter where. No doubt I could learn something from the right side of the highway too.

This Tuesday morning—one of those perfect fall days New Brunswick should bottle and sell, clear, sunny and warm with the sky a shade of blue so rich that if your prints came back from the processors that colour you would return them as phony—I was canvassing in the ritziest neighbourhood in our mainly working-class riding. Poll 25, it said on my kit, Imperial Drive and Royal Crescent. The houses here were all big, some old established homes, mostly on Imperial, and some expensive new places. I left my truck, with its campaign signs to take advantage of the free advertising at the busy junction of Imperial and the highway, and set off on what I knew was a pretty useless task. At least it wasn't raining, like the day I did the trailer park the week before, when every slobbering, muddy-pawed dog that each trailer seemed to

have two of fell in love with me. Mind you, I got fourteen
sign locations there—I suppose the dogs would be as
pleased with those as I was. I found it hard to imagine
the expensive lawns down here flourishing "Vote Drabble,
N.D.P." signs. They didn't even allow conservative dan-
delions.

Imperial Drive was technically on the river—it was
really a bay here, about four miles across and twenty miles
long—but the grounds of the houses were so extensive
that you only had the odd glimpse of the water and the
hills on the other side through the carefully spaced Scotch
pines and red maples on the lush, level turf. It was the
older houses which dominated the waterfront; the more
recent arrivals to affluence were relegated to the other side
of the drive on lots which, although they were carved out
of reclaimed spruce-bogs, would have cost ten times as
much as one of the old places would have gone for, fifty
years before. That would have been lot and house and all.

I decided to try the river side first, figuring that I'd be
more likely to find people at home there. Nearly everyone
would be out at work on the other side, earning the two
big incomes they would need to keep up their mortgage
payments. Number 5—I had no idea what had become of
1 and 3—was the first one on my list, the home of Edward
George Anstruther, Retired Businessman, and Eleanor
Jane Anstruther, Housekeeper. Through impressive stone
gateposts there was an elegant driveway of clean, pink
gravel; bordered by rhododendrons, it curved round a meticulously cared-for lawn to the porch of a classic brown,
two-storey house. While I might have gone round to the
back door of a farmhouse this size, out in the rural part
of the riding, I would be damned if I was going to the
kitchen entrance here. There was a big brass knocker on
the heavy door, but it looked as if it was purely cere-
monial, for not a fingerprint had sullied its polished lion's

head. To the side of the door was a doorbell, set also in a bright ring of brass, and when I pushed this there was an impressive, almost ecclesiastical chime from the hallway inside.

I waited, rechecking the name of the household on the voters list on my clip-board. The Anstruthers were a well-known family, Tories probably. The garden really was gigantic, with colourful flower beds even this late in the season in neat symmetrical array patterning the lawn, and as I was admiring it, the door behind me swished open. "Good morning, Mr. Anstruther," I said smiling to a real dignified-looking old guy, wearing gold, half-frame glasses, and leather slippers. The rest of his clothing was casual and elegant at the same time, in the way that only very well-heeled people with old money seem to be able to manage; something to do with self-assurance, I suppose, and never having to impress anyone. He was holding a newspaper, too, not the local paper but one of those thin airmail editions of some English paper. It rustled funny in the breeze at the door. "I'm Walter Drabble, the NDP candidate, just making some calls in the neighbourhood." He smiled a kind of condescending smile. It struck me right then that he likely wouldn't take kindly to me calling Imperial Drive a "neighbourhood." "Pleased to meet you, Mr. Drabble," he said, shaking my offered hand. "I don't think we've ever had one of you people round this way before. So nice of you to call." The way he said "you people" made me feel I was on day-parole from the mental hospital. "Yeah, well, I suppose most of the people around here have made up their minds already," I said, trying not to sound too offensive, "but I—" Another smile, like the kind royal visitors wear in day-care centres, interrupted me. "Now, don't you be so sure of that, Mr. Drabble. Some of us may still have open minds." I'd be lucky not to be kept in after class. We chatted for a while, friendly enough, and as I was turning to go I handed him the leaflet with my photograph on the front. Come to think of it, it did make me look as though I was on day-parole from somewhere. The cheap printing of the photograph and the typesetting—we couldn't afford colour—was vaguely reminiscent of Post Office walls. "Thank you so much for calling, it's been a pleasure talking to you, Mr. Drabble. We'll certainly read your pamphlets with the greatest interest. Good luck in your canvassing." At least he didn't add "anyway," the usual deadening dismissal. But he didn't have to be so blatant. On the way back down between the rhododendrons, I marked an "X" for "definitely not" opposite his name under the First Canvass column on my sheet. In fact I marked two "X"s, figuring there wasn't much hope for his wife, Mrs. Eleanor J., either. No doubt they would vote as partners.

That was the way it went down most of that side, except for a couple of places that were "Not Homes"—off to South Carolina likely, for the winter—every one was a more-or-less polite and condescending "X." I think I would have preferred a couple of rude arguments, or some thinly-veiled fascism, overt support for South Africa or chain gangs for the unemployed (I'd relished a few of these elsewhere on my rounds) but all I got was ever so genteel dismissal. Until I got to the end house, a rambling old place, not nearly as well cared for as the others, with the green paint peeling from the door frame and windows, and the big garden mostly overgrown with alders. The drapes at the side of the dirty bay windows were of faded brown velvet, and hung crazily, with several of their hooks detached. The button on the doorbell was permanently pushed in and for a while there was no answer to my knock, but just as I was about to slide a folded leaflet in between the loose draught-proofing and the door, a vigorous, cheerful voice called from inside. "Who is it? I shan't be a minute." I tried to explain as well as I could what my business was; I daresay I'd have shouted through the keyhole if there had been one. When she eventually opened the door, I was surprised to see a tall woman of about seventy or so, with wispy, kind of wild, white hair, under a bright orange head-scarf tied up in a turban; she was wearing an almost fluorescent housecoat of lime-green with a bold purple pattern of flowers, and tatty black-and-white Adidas running shoes, their laces untied. The voice, I could now make out, was Welsh, and wonder of wonders, she recognized me.

"Mr. Drabble! I wondered if the NDP would be round." She didn't speak, she sang. "You see I have something *very* important to tell you that you can use to dev-a-stating effect in your campaign." My heart sank. I'd heard too many earth-shaking revelations in the past couple of weeks to be impressed anymore. Some days every third voter knew something, it seemed, that would destroy the government or the official opposition, and be sure to have me elected, if I would just use it right. They knew scandals, they told me about them in great detail; they knew of someone's daughter who lost her job through unfair influence; they knew of some shady deal between a major industrialist and the sitting member; they had clear evidence of corruption in the enumeration; one old guy up in the trailer park said he knew somebody whose brother worked for a man whose wife was sleeping with the present M.L.A. (he was more the laying member than the sitting member, it seemed, or maybe the standing member). I always listened politely—well, you never know—but I hadn't heard anything yet that was more than just rumour, and mostly third- or fourth-hand. Even though hers was to be dev-a-stating, I didn't hold out much hope for its usefulness.

For the first time that morning I was invited past the door, and offered a seat. The house was as much of a mess inside as it was out, with books and papers on every chair. On shelves and dressers around the big parlour there were dusty mementoes of what looked like extensive travel: some African carvings in ebony, copper vases, several expensive-looking Inuit soapstone pieces; on the walls there was a strange mixture of original oils in startling colours and expensive-looking antique prints of Old Quebec. Above a cluttered desk in one corner there was a five-foot-by-four-foot survey map of New Brunswick. There was only one name on the voters roll for this address, so I guessed Mrs. Megan Flewelling was a widow. "Now I don't suppose you have too much time, Mr. Drabble"— this was encouraging, at any rate; mostly people on their own wanted to keep me all day— "so I'll get to the point. You've probably heard of my late husband, David Flewelling, he was the most prominent chemical engineer in Canada before he died." I hadn't, but I gave a non-committal nod in response. "Yes, I was sure you would have. He was the senior man in all Rhodesia, as it was then, before we came here." As she went on with a weird story of industrial espionage, and government deceit, I was first of all interested and then increasingly skeptical and uncomfortable. Her improbable story flitted from East Africa—"I'm going to write the story of my life some day, you know, Walter—I can call you Walter, can't I—I shot a man once you know, in Bulawayo. A German miner, he was, broke into our house when David was away. I really gave the bugger a fright, with the old Mauser David made me keep in the bedside table drawer. Blew a hole in his shoulder you could have put your fist through. Still have that gun somewhere. He made sure I could use it, too—I was a crack shot then." As opposed, I thought, to being just plain cracked, now. To Northern Quebec—"I used to be fluent in French, in those days, David made sure I had the best lessons, with my Welsh accent, they used to say I sounded like a Métis." In New Brunswick, she said, David had devised a new process for making paper from any kind of waste-wood, but the big lumber companies had all ganged up on him to keep it secret. "I've been going over David's manuscripts—I know a good deal about chemistry myself, you know, couldn't help picking it up over the years—and when I have them all together I'll give you permission to use them. It'll blow the lid off the whole conspiracy, really it will." Her voice had the fierce conviction and total clarity that only the really crazy can master; as she spoke she twirled round her elegant fingers a wisp of hair at her neck, underneath the turban. When I rose to go, she promised she would phone the office when the report was ready, and would also like to make a sub-stan-tial contribution to the cause, whenever she could find her cheque book. I gave her the leaflet with the campaign-office address and telephone number; she would phone, all right, at great length and late at night, likely, but I was not so sure about the cheque.

As I suspected, most of the houses on the other side of the street were empty, and I had six N/H marks for "Not Home" on my canvass sheet before long. I usually resented spending time in polls like this, but the morning was so bright and warm that I was really enjoying the lengthy walks between each driveway. The seventh house was a large half-timbered structure in an ornate version of Contractor's Tudor; it was obviously new, for the expensive, freshly-turfed lawn still faintly showed the lines where it had been unrolled; and on a short, steep banking by the side of the driveway there were wooden pegs like some primitive hairpins holding squares of turf in place. It gave the place a kind of temporary look, as though the people who lived here were really just part of a display, and were ready to move on when the show was over. You couldn't call the entrance a porch; it was a portico. It was that grand, with elaborate glass panels set in a rich, shiny wood, and a profusion of brass trim around bell, handle and lock; it occurred to me that it probably cost more than most of the houses in the poorer parts of the riding. There was a delicate, exotic perfume in the air which I couldn't define—though the name on the long, polished plate under the bell gave me a clue—Dr. M.V. Besse-Patel, M.D; M.R.C.P; F.R.C.S. When I leaned on the button, the chimes inside played the first thirteen notes of "Be it ever so humble, there's no place like home."

I was trying hard to hide my laughter when the door opened. "Good morning, may I help you?" The slight woman standing in the door was beautiful and serene, with dark, shiny hair, and eyes like chestnuts; her sari floated around her like a cinnamon-and-lemon cloud, but the voice was so perfectly Oxford that my mirth overcame me again. I could only stammer out my introduction, before the giggles took control.

"Do you find something amusing, Mr. Drabble?" she asked, not in any defensive way, but in the sure confidence that it could not possibly be anything in her house or appearance that would be amusing to me.

"No," I lied, desperately searching for a grip, "I'm so sorry, it was something from earlier this morning that just came back to me." Holding my clip-board and leaflets between my knees, I made a pretence of wiping my glasses on my tie, to give me time to control the hysteria. She showed remarkable restraint, giving no sign that she noticed how ludicrous I must have looked.

"I see your name is not on the voters list—Mrs. Patel, is it?" She nodded graciously. "It is Besse-Patel, actually, and I also am a doctor. We do not meet the residential requirements, by virtue of our short time here. My husband is not at home this morning." My own English suddenly felt totally inadequate—somehow a B.A. from Mount Allison seemed a bit shabby. Over her shoulder I could see a sumptuously carpeted hallway, its walls bright with opulent prints of oriental lovers, acrobatically entwined. "If he were home, however, he would be delighted to speak to you; he has a deep love of politics." Yeah, I thought, I just bet he has. "When we were students in England, we used to be active workers for the Labour Party, you see." That made me become serious with a real start. In this palace? That would likely have been when they were young and foolish, which was how some former socialists explained their lapse of faith. No heart if you are not a socialist at twenty, no brain if you are still one at thirty, wasn't that how it went? "Well, isn't that interesting. And what about now, are you both still active? We could use some good campaign workers, if you could spare us a few hours—even if you can't vote yet, I mean."

She smiled a sweet, condescending smile. "Oh no, I do not think that would be appropriate, with my husband's position at the hospital. But I shall take your leaflet, and be sure that he reads it. I have no doubt when we obtain our citizenship we shall vote for your party." She took the pamphlet from me delicately; it seemed incredible that, even in younger, more foolish days, such fingers had ever been stained with cheap printer's ink.

Be it ever so humble, indeed. I marked off a "Not Eligible" on my sheet beside the written-in name and address, along with a note to have someone in the fundraising committee give them a call. I hummed the tune as I walked back to the truck, thinking what a good story it would make at the canvass wrap-up that night. And them on Imperial Drive, too. I was laughing out loud all the way back to the Best For Less to give Karen my canvassing report.

Karen was on time for a change, or maybe I was late; she was sitting at a small table at the back. She was working on the proofs of a new pamphlet spread out in front of her and they were in danger of either being swamped by her coffee—did you ever know of coffee in a styrofoam cup not ending up over the most important papers on the table?—or being set alight by the cigarette-ends smouldering in the foil ash-tray. She looked up as I sat down, her eyes huge behind the curved lenses. There was in them that characteristic intensity that the part of me that didn't make fun of, envied.

"Hi," she said, so that I didn't know whether it was a greeting or a sigh. "How'd it go this morning?" I told her, leaving out No Place like Home. I wanted to keep that for an audience that would be more appreciative.

"Yeah, I was looking over those phone responses again; it was poll 35 that looked good, not 25. 25's a wash out. Sorry. You've just been wasting your time all morning. And I think so have I—look at the mess the printer made of the copy I gave him." Maybe she had fouled up the phone-canvass results, but she sure knew her stuff when it came to putting pamphlets together. As she went over the lay-out with me, pointing with her pencil to the places where the printer had the proportions wrong, and where the placement of the photographs wasn't quite right, I was grateful, not for the first time, for her specialised knowledge in that strange line of work. Maybe she was right, and I was just wasting my time. But remembering the morning's visits I couldn't bring myself to think so. No, even if I had been in the wrong poll, I hadn't been wasting my time at all.